Gourmet Holiday Murder

Book Six

in

Papa Pacelli's

Pizzeria Series

By

Patti Benning

ISBN:

Author's Note: On the next page, you'll find out how to access all of my books easily, as well as locate books by best-selling author, Summer Prescott. I'd love to hear your thoughts on my books, the storylines, and anything else that you'd like to comment on – reader feedback is very important to me. Please see the following page for my publisher's contact information. If you'd like to be on her list of "folks to contact" with updates, release and sales notifications, etc…just shoot her an email and let her know. Thanks for reading!

Also…

…if you're looking for more great reads, from me and Summer, check out the Summer Prescott Publishing Book Catalog:

http://summerprescottbooks.com/book-catalog/ for some truly delicious stories.

Contact Info for Summer Prescott Publishing:

Twitter: @summerprescott1

Blog and Book Catalog: http://summerprescottbooks.com

Email: summer.prescott.cozies@gmail.com

And…look up The Summer Prescott Fan Page on Facebook – let's be friends!

If you're an author and are interested in publishing with Summer Prescott Books – please send Summer an email and she'll send you submission guidelines.

TABLE OF CONTENTS

GOURMET HOLIDAY
MURDER

Book Six in Papa Pacelli's Pizzeria Series

CHAPTER ONE

Eleanora Pacelli pulled her hat down more tightly on her head, partly to hide the faint bruise from her fall off a roof a couple weeks ago, but mainly to keep the icy wind from biting at her ears. December had hit northern Maine with a vengeance, and the warm days of summer already seemed like a faraway dream.

"So, what do you think?" she asked, shoving her hands deep into her jacket pockets as another gust of wind assaulted her. Powdery snow lifted from the ground and blew across the sidewalk in front of her.

"You're sure you don't want to wait until spring to do this?" the contractor asked. George Walsh was a tall, thin man with a slightly threadbare jacket. He had a habit of tapping his fingers together that Ellie found not annoying, exactly, but distracting. They were standing behind the pizzeria, near the employee entrance, gazing at the back wall, a wall that Ellie felt she now knew as well as the back of her own hand.

Ellie nodded. "I think a drive-up window will help keep sales up even when it's freezing out. The way things are set up now, people either have to park in the back and walk all the way around the block to the front entrance, or try to find a spot to park along Main Street. No one wants to walk further than they have to when it's cold. This way, customers will be able to drive right up to the window and pick up their pizza without leaving their car."

"Well, it's doable," he said, giving the brick wall next to the employee entrance an appraising look. "It's going to cost you more right now, though, it being the off season and all. It would be less expensive for you to schedule something for the spring or summer."

"I know, but I think it will give our sales a bump over the winter," Ellie said, biting back a sigh. She didn't have to justify herself to this man. All she wanted was an estimate. "My hope is that it pays for itself by spring. I've already got estimates from a few contractors. You're actually the last I'm seeing before I make a decision, so it shouldn't take long for me to get back to you."

"Right, well I can give you a rough quote now. You're probably looking at least…" he told her the number. Ellie nodded. It wasn't the highest she had heard over the last few days, but it wasn't the lowest either. Of course, she wanted to make sure that work that she was getting done was quality work, so she wouldn't be making her decision solely on the quoted price. Mr. Walsh was still in the running.

"Thanks," she told him. "I'll give you a call by tomorrow evening, all right? I'll let you know either way. I really appreciate you meeting me out here on such short notice like this."

"Thank *you* for considering my company," he said, shaking her hand. "I look forward to hearing from you, Ms. Pacelli."

Ellie went back inside the building with relief. It was already freezing outside, even though winter didn't officially start for another couple of weeks. She was not looking forward to the frigid weather of late December and January. *Why couldn't Nonna have lived somewhere warm? If only she and Papa had decided to retire somewhere nice, like most people, then I could be running a pizza shop in Florida right now…*

Still, she couldn't complain. Just months ago, she had lost everything—her fiancé, her apartment, and the career she had worked so hard for over half her adult life. She had thought that she had hit rock bottom, but had another dose of bad news when she found out that her paternal grandfather had died. Her move back to Maine to care for her elderly and now-alone grandmother, however, had been a blessing in disguise. She was glad that she was getting the chance to spend time with Nonna, even if it just made her regret even more her distance from this side of her family for so many years.

Spending time with Nonna wasn't the only good thing that had come of her return to Kittiport. She had been handed a full-time job—managing the pizzeria—on a silver platter, and just weeks ago had been given full legal control of the restaurant by her grandmother. It was still hard to believe that she was a business owner. The addition of a drive-up window was her way of trying to make it all seem real. It was her first major change as the new owner of Papa Pacelli's. She just hoped that it didn't end up being a flop.

"How'd it go?" one of her employees asked as she shut the door behind her.

"The price he gave me was about mid-range," she told him as she pulled off her hat. "I'm going to have to take a look at his website again, and see if I can find any reviews about him online. I think it's a tie between him and that guy we had in yesterday."

Jacob Stevens was a lanky young man who had been working at the pizzeria for longer than Ellie had been there. At the moment, he was busy mixing up another batch of pizza dough—an endless task that any of them could do with their eyes closed.

"The one who said this place has the best pizza he'd ever eaten in his life?" he asked.

"That's the one." Ellie grinned, remembering. "Really, it's the fact that he said he hates Cheesaroni Calzones that won me over. Anyone who doesn't like them has got to be a good guy."

Cheesaroni Calzones was her main competition in town. The man who owned it, Jeffrey Dunham, had hated her since the moment they met, and had tried to sabotage the pizzeria a few times in the past. His right-hand man, Xavier Hurst, had once been Papa Pacelli's manager; Ellie had fired him when she discovered that he had stolen thousands of dollars from her grandfather. As far as she was concerned, someone who shared her dislike of the two men deserved the benefit of the doubt.

"Did I hear someone mention Cheesaroni?" asked a young woman who had just pushed through the door to the kitchen. Iris was the newest addition to the team at the pizzeria, and Ellie was still getting used to her outlandish sense of style. Today, her short hair was dark red with bright purple tips, and her chipped nail polish was a bilious neon green. She looked like she belonged in a dance club, not a family-friendly pizza restaurant, but she had a bubbly energy and an earnestness that Ellie had immediately taken to. So far, she hadn't had any reason to regret hiring the woman.

"We were just talking about how Ms. Pacelli's probably going to hire the guy who said he didn't like them," Jacob told her, going back to his dough.

"Well, he also gave me the second lowest quote," Ellie said a bit defensively. "The one who had the lowest quote never called me back after I asked for references, so I'm not going to take a chance on him."

"When do you think construction will start?" Iris asked as she washed her hands at the sink.

"I'm hoping sometime next week," the pizzeria owner told her. "It shouldn't take too long; they're just cutting a window in the side of the building, installing some glass, and putting an awning up. We'll probably have to shut down for two days at the most." She wasn't even going to try to keep the pizzeria up and running while the construction company was working on the window. She doubted her employees would want to work with a gaping hole in one of the kitchen walls, not to mention the fact that getting drywall dust all over the pizzas wouldn't exactly help the restaurant's reputation. It would be nice to take a few days off and spend some time at home with the woman who had made all this possible.

Ellie's grandmother, Ann Pacelli, had inspired her to install the window. She was still wearing a sling for her broken arm, and had complained about how difficult it was for her to carry out pizzas one-handed. Jokingly, Ellie had suggested that they install a drive-through window to make it easier for her, but the idea had taken hold and seemed to grow on its own. She was toying with the idea of adding an outdoor eating area as well, but that could wait until summer. For now, all she wanted was to make it as easy as possible for her customers to pick up pizzas during the frigid Maine winter. Her goal was to exceed her grandfather's sales record by midsummer. From there, who knew where the pizzeria would go?

As the sun sank in the sky and Papa Pacelli's began to draw in more customers as people got off work, Ellie pushed the upcoming construction project out of her mind and turned her thoughts instead to what she was going to do for Christmas. She felt torn between her grandmother and her mother. The latter had left her a voicemail inviting her back to the Midwest to spend the holidays at her house. She was tempted to go, but she knew that would likely mean leaving her grandmother behind to celebrate Christmas on her own. Though Nonna had invited both of her children to come over for dinner on Christmas Eve, Ellie doubted that either would show up.

It was a tough decision to make, but in the end, she knew that she wouldn't be able to leave her grandmother alone over the holidays. Besides the fact that she firmly believed no one should be alone over Christmas, the memory of Nonna's fall down the stairs a few weeks ago was still fresh in her head. Even with the older woman's friends checking on her, there would be too much opportunity for something similar to happen while no one was there. Still, she wasn't looking forward to her calling her mother back with the news that she wasn't coming over for Christmas.

"I'll have to figure something else out for next year," she muttered as she slid a bacon and spinach pizza onto a platter for one of their eat-in customers. "Life is never simple."

"Huh? Sorry, Ms. P., I didn't catch that," Jacob said. He had just come in from a delivery, and was shrugging off a snowy jacket.

"Just talking to myself, Jacob," she said. "Did it start snowing again?" She knew the road out to the Pacelli house likely wouldn't be plowed until morning. Hopefully her little car would be able to make it home without sliding into a ditch. The cellphone service out there was spotty enough that she didn't like her chances of getting rescued.

"It's just the wind kicking snow up," he said. "The sky's clear, but the snow is drifting onto the road. I'm not looking forward to taking the next delivery out."

"I can tell Iris to stop taking delivery orders, if you don't feel safe driving in this weather," Ellie offered. "The last thing I want is for you to get in an accident."

He considered it for a moment, then shook his head. "Thanks for offering, but I'll be fine. The weather's going to get a lot worse this winter. Plus, I could use the tips."

By the time Ellie brought the spinach and bacon pizza out to her guests, she had a whole new set of worries resting on her shoulders. She didn't like the idea of sending her employees out to deliver pizzas when the roads were dangerous. She would have to look into creating a new policy—maybe she would stop all deliveries if there was more than a certain number of inches of snow on the ground, or during winter weather warnings. She was responsible for her employees' safety, and knew she would never forgive herself if something happened to one of them on her watch.

"One large thin-crust bacon and spinach pizza with white sauce," she said as she set the pizza tray down on the table. "Is there anything else I can get you?"

"I think this is it, thanks." The middle-aged woman smiled as her teenage daughter pulled a slice of pizza off of the platter. "I love what you've done with this place. The Christmas decorations are gorgeous, though I do miss those little turkeys you had on the tables over Thanksgiving."

"Thanks. I love decorating for the holidays," Ellie said with a smile. "It can be a lot of work, but I think it really helps get people in the mood to celebrate."

She paused on the way back to the kitchen and admired the pizzeria, trying to see it as her customers did. There were green, red, and white Christmas lights lining the display window at the front of the room, as well as a strand of lights along the edge of the counter where the register sat. A fake tree that had been decorated by her employees took up the corner next to the soda fridge, and she had small figurines of Santa and his reindeer on each of the tables.

My home away from home, she thought, feeling a burst of affection for the pizzeria. Running the place wasn't always easy, but it was definitely worth it.

CHAPTER TWO

The Pacelli house was a big colonial to the north of town. It faced the coast, and sat at the edge of a state park. With the ocean in front of it, and tall pines behind it, Ellie was constantly surrounded by as much nature as she could ever want. Truth be told, she could have done without the dark, looming trees and the bitterly cold sea winds, but there was something to be said for the privacy and peace that came with living away from town.

The interior of the house was clean and well decorated, and right now smelled of reheated Thanksgiving food. Bunny, Ellie's black-and-white papillon, was staring up at an old woman sitting hunched over her food at the breakfast nook in the kitchen, while Ellie took a plate out of the microwave.

"I never thought I'd be tired of turkey and stuffing," Ellie said. "But I'm getting there. You cooked for an army, Nonna."

"Well, I didn't want all of the food that I bought to go to waste. If I had known that you would spend the holiday in the hospital, I would have only bought enough groceries for the two of us."

"I can't complain. It's good cooking." Ellie took a seat next to the older woman, doing her best to ignore Bunny, who was now gazing up at her hopefully.

"How is the work on the pizzeria coming?" Nonna asked.

"Not bad. I decided which contractor to use yesterday. The work should start soon."

"Isn't your friend's husband a contractor?"

Ellie knew she meant James Ward, who was married to her best friend Shannon. She had gone on a couple dates with his brother, the sheriff. Russell Ward couldn't have been more different from James, and she found it easy to forget the two were related. They might not have looked much like brothers, but they were both good men to the core.

"James is a contractor, but he just accepted a big job. Shannon offered to tell him I was looking for someone, but I didn't want to bother him. It's just a little window that needs to be put in. He's so nice, that I know he would offer to do it, but I'm sure he's got more important things on his plate."

"That's very thoughtful of you," Nonna said, giving her hand a pat. "You're such a kind person, Ellie. I don't know what I'd do without you. I really appreciate you coming to stay here with me. I don't think I say that enough."

"Well, I'm happy to be here," Ellie said. It was true. Returning to Kittiport had been like coming home after a long vacation. The little town on the coast of Maine was where she belonged; she felt it in her heart.

After lunch, the older woman retired to her room and Ellie did something she had never done before; she clipped the leash onto Bunny's collar, got into her car, and drove to the nearest entrance to the state park that bordered her grandmother's property. It was a beautiful day—clear and still, with the sun glittering off snow-covered trees—and she wanted to enjoy it to the fullest.

"This will be good for both of us," she told her dog as they got out of the car. She paused to straighten her scarf. With no wind, it wasn't as bitingly cold as it had been the last couple of days, but it was still far below freezing. "We haven't been getting out enough, now that it's dark whenever I come home from work."

She began walking briskly down the nearest path, the frozen leaves under the snow crunching with each step. There were a few other vehicles in the parking lot, and she could hear children laughing off in the distance. It was reassuring to know that she wasn't alone in the forest. She was a city girl; all of this nature was far more intimidating than busy urban streets ever were.

After a good half hour of following the path, Ellie was feeling decidedly toasty. Her breath steamed out in front of her, and she even unzipped her coat partway to let cool air in as she watched her dog romp through the snow.

Bunny was having the time of her life. Ellie had bought her a sweater for the cold weather, but the papillon hardly seemed to need it. As she watched, the little dog buried her face in a snow drift, then gave a big snort and jumped back. They had rarely gone on excursions like this back when they had lived in Chicago; most of their walks had taken place along busy streets.

"We'll have to do this more often, girl," she said aloud to the dog. Her voice sounded strangely loud. She realized that she couldn't hear the children shouting and laughing in the distance any more. How were the woods *so* quiet? Where was the birdsong? There was no sound but for the occasional creak of one of the tall pines in the breeze and the crunch of snow under her feet and Bunny's paws.

Beginning to feel uncomfortable at just how alone she was out there, she cleared her throat and tightened her grip on Bunny's leash. "It's time to go back, girl. Maybe we can come out again later this week. I'll see if Russell wants to join us, too. He likes all of this nature stuff."

She got them turned around and let Bunny run out in front of her again. The little dog proved just as enthusiastic about retracing their steps, and zig-zagged across the path, sniffing everything she could reach. Ellie let her mind wander, thinking about her plans for the pizzeria. It was doing well now, there was no denying that, but the competitive streak in her wanted it to do even *better.* In her far-off fantasies, she imagined Papa Pacelli's as a nationwide chain, serving the best pizza in the country.

They weren't quite at that point yet, but she was still extremely proud of how far they had come. When she had first arrived in Kittiport and had taken over the pizzeria, it had been struggling along on its last legs. Just as she had gotten her own fresh start, Papa Pacelli's had gotten a second chance as well. She knew, however, that she couldn't take responsibility for all of their recent success. A lot of the restaurant's new image had to do with how dedicated her employees were. She had given them each a chance to leave after she had fired Xavier, and they had all decided not just to stay, but to work hard to improve the restaurant's image. That meant a lot to her.

"I should do something nice for them for Christmas," she said to Bunny, who ignored her. "What sorts of gifts would it be okay to give my employees?"

She was still considering that question as she returned to the parking lot and got into her car. Bunny spun around once, then lay down on the passenger seat. Ellie started the engine and let it warm up while she thought. She could get them gift cards, but that seemed too impersonal. Of course, they probably wouldn't want gifts that were *too* personal from her; she was their boss, after all.

"I've got to find something for Shannon, Russell, and Nonna too," she sighed. "I wish you could talk, Bunny. You'd probably have some good ideas."

The little dog's tail thumped against the seat at the sound of her name, then the papillon yawned and tucked her nose under a paw. It was time for a nap.

At home, Ellie warmed up with a glass of vanilla tea before tackling the job of putting up the Christmas lights. Nonna had boxes of the things in the basement, and probably even more in the attic, though no one had been up there in years. The big pine tree out front was just begging to be done up. Ellie had been prepared to start the project the day after she got home from the hospital, but Russell had talked her into waiting until he could help her… or at the very least, until her headache went away. She agreed with him that tall ladders and concussions didn't go well together, but she wasn't prepared to wait for his help. While she was grateful that he had offered, she knew it could be days until he was able to get away from the sheriff's department for long enough to get the lights up. Patience wasn't her foremost virtue, and since she had been blessedly headache free for the past two days, she decided to go ahead with the project on her own.

After dragging the dusty boxes up from the basement, she pulled out and untangled the strands of lights. There was a good variety, and while she was tempted to use the flashing red and green lights on the outdoor tree, she decided to go with the pale blue lights instead. She could leave them up all winter, since the color wasn't strictly holiday themed.

Ellie carried the lights outside and set them on a tarp in the snow, then unlocked the garage and pushed her way inside. She didn't know how long it had been since the building had been used for cars. Right now, it was full to the brim of old tools and appliances, cardboard boxes, and antique furniture. *I need to talk to Nonna about getting this place cleaned out*, she said. *We can probably sell a lot of this to an antique shop.* She pushed past an old rocking chair and took a heavy extension cord off the workbench. Her eyes landed on an extendible ladder on the other side of the garage. That would be perfect, if she could ever get it out.

Half an hour later, Ellie was at the top of the big pine tree out front, slowly winding the lights around the branches while her grandmother and a neighbor, who had been kind enough to come help when he had seen what they were doing, held onto the ladder from below. She was beginning to realize that this job *would* be a lot easier for two people to do—one on each side of the tree. She was making do, though, and she could already tell that when she was finished, the effect would be gorgeous.

"There, it's finished," Ellie said, stepping off the ladder for the final time. Her hands were sticky with tree sap, but she didn't mind the sharp pine scent that clung to them. "Where's the end of the extension cord?"

Nonna handed her the cord, and Ellie pulled the end of the last strand of lights down from the lowest branch and plugged it in. She had already tested all of the lights before putting them on the tree, but she still felt a tingle of relief when the entire tree lit up with no issues.

"Look at that," Nonna said, taking a step back so she could admire the entire image. "You did a wonderful job, Ellie."

"Thanks, Nonna." It had been hard work, but she was glad it was done. She couldn't wait until it got dark. The tree would really stand out then.

"I'm really looking forward to Christmas this year," her grandmother said. "With you in the house, it will be just like old times."

CHAPTER THREE

Dating a sheriff wasn't easy, especially when that sheriff was Russell Ward. One of the things that had originally drawn Ellie to him was the fact that he took his job so seriously. He never cut corners and never overlooked a suspect, even if he knew them personally. Sometimes that meant he had to make hard choices, like arresting his best friend for murder. Other times that meant cancelling dates at the last minute because of emergency calls. Between his job and hers, it was rare to have a whole uninterrupted evening together.

Luckily, they were both happy to take their relationship slowly. Their dates remained casual, and they talked about all manner of things from work to their families. Ellie was beginning to feel for the first time in her life like she was building a relationship with a man that was based solidly in friendship and respect. It was hard to think now of her years putting up with her ex-fiancé's antics. Kittiport had changed her a lot in the months since she had moved back, and most of those changes were for the better.

Even though there was the risk of one of them having to leave to deal with one emergency or another at their jobs, Ellie always looked forward to going out with Russell. When he called the next day to tell her he had the evening off, she jumped at the chance to have him over. Putting the lights on the tree had been one thing, but she wasn't prepared to begin putting the icicle lights along the gutters without an able-bodied someone there to help.

A few hours after his phone call, Russell's arrival was announced by a smattering of happy yaps from Bunny, who could recognize the sound of his truck from a block away. Ellie spared one last glance in the hall mirror on her way to answer the door and gave herself an encouraging smile. Her hair, which was straight and dark and refused to do anything more than just hang there, was up in a ponytail and out of the way. She was wearing her favorite blouse and jeans combo, and had a gorgeous handknit wool scarf hanging on the coat hook by the door along with her jacket.

Of course, she doubted that Russell cared what she wore. He had seen her tear-streaked and covered in someone else's blood—nearly anything would be an improvement to that. Still, it mattered to *her.* She had always believed that if something was important to her, she should put her best foot forward. And she did care about her relationship with Russell, despite the fact that she wasn't quite sure how she had managed to end up in the relationship in the first place. All of her promises to herself that she wouldn't let a man distract her from her career goals again had seemed to just float away when she'd started spending more time with him.

"Back up," Ellie said, nudging Bunny out of the way with her leg as she reached for the door. "You're not allowed out front without a leash anymore."

Just a few days ago, the dog had dashed out the door and into the road when Ellie was getting home from work. It had been snowing, so the road wasn't as easy to see as it normally was. The incident still frightened her, and she didn't want to chance it happening again until she had time to work with Bunny a little more on recall training.

She got the door open and, blocking Bunny with her legs, greeted Russell with a smile. He looked more relaxed than usual when he smiled back.

"I brought you a coffee," he said, holding up two steaming paper cups.

"Not from the sheriff's department?"

"Nope." He grinned. The sheriff's department had notoriously bad coffee. Ellie didn't know what it was; she had even tried her hand at making some herself once, and it had turned out just as bad as always. *Maybe I should get them a new coffee maker for Christmas,* she thought. *Though come to think of it, that might put the coffee shop around the block out of business.*

"My favorite," she laughed. She took the cup that he offered her, and stepped back, inviting him in while keeping Bunny firmly blocked from the door.

The little dog was thrilled to see the sheriff. Once Ellie released her, the papillon bounced around the two of them, her tail a blur. Russell crouched down to her level and withdrew a bag of treats from his pocket. He kept them there in case he had to deal with dogs in the course of his work, but they worked very well for bribing Bunny as well.

"I didn't forget about you, little girl," he said. "I've got your cookies. Here you go."

Ellie smiled as she watched the two of them interact. Russell seemed more like a German shepherd guy to her, but he always made a point to do something nice for the little papillon. She was struck, not for the first time, by what a genuinely good man he was.

"I see you put the lights up on the tree already," he said when he straightened up. He raised an eyebrow. "I know you don't have to listen to me when I tell you to be careful, but even the doctor said you should avoid heights for a while."

"I felt fine, and Nonna and a neighbor spotted me," she told him. "The lights got up without a hitch."

"You could have just waited for me," he said. "You know I worry about you. You're a bit… accident prone."

"I don't usually fall off roofs," she remarked. "It was a one-time thing. Anyway, I didn't know when you'd have time to stop by and help."

He shrugged in concession. "Fair enough, things at the department these past few months have been crazier than usual. I don't want to jinx it, but things have really slowed down this week. I'm hoping everything stays nice and calm through the holidays."

"I hope so too," Ellie said. "I really do. You need a break from the insanity."

"Well, I knew what I was getting into when I ran for sheriff. I can't complain." He rubbed the back of his neck and looked around. "Where's your grandmother?" Russell had known the elder Pacellis for years, and never failed to greet Ellie's nonna if she was around.

"One of her friends picked her up an hour ago. They're going Christmas shopping. I was strictly forbidden from going with them."

Russell chuckled. "I wonder what she's getting you?"

"I have no idea," Ellie said. "She already gave me the pizzeria. As far as I'm concerned, I've already got everything I could ever want."

"How's that going, anyway? Did you start the renovations yet?"

"The work starts Tuesday evening. We're closing early that day, and opening late on Thursday, which is when the contractor said they should be finished."

"That's quick," he said.

"Well, it's a pretty simple project," she said. "They're just going to knock a hole through the wall and put a window in. Maybe it's not as simple as that, but it's the gist of it. Putting in the outdoor eating area next summer will take a lot longer, but we shouldn't need to close down for that."

"I can't wait for that," he said. "Nothing beats eating outside on a nice summer day with a steady breeze from the ocean coming in."

They both looked outside to where the ground was white and the ocean was visible as a steely grey line in the distance. Summer was a long way off.

Taking advantage of Russell's help while she could, Ellie pulled on her scarf and jacket and they got to work on the rest of the outdoor decorations. Gradually, the house began to look more festive. While the sheriff put up the icicle lights along the gutter, she put a wreath on the door and sorted out the rest of the decorations that she planned to use.

By the time they had finished putting up the outdoor decorations, Ellie's fingers and toes were freezing. She and Russell took a few moments to admire their work, then went inside to warm up. The sheriff was still in an unusually good mood, and she wondered whether it was just the fact that things had been slower at the department lately, or if there was something else. She got her answer as they sat at the kitchen table and sipped some of the butterscotch cocoa that she'd made.

"You know, I forgot how much I missed all of this," he said.

"All of this…? You mean Christmas stuff?"

He nodded. "I haven't really done anything for the holidays for the past few years, besides whatever meals James and Shannon invite me to. It's good to get away from work for a bit and do normal Christmas things."

Ellie wondered if he had stopped doing stuff for Christmas after his wife had died. He never spoke much about her, and she never asked. Maybe it was just hard to get into the holidays when most of your time was spent dealing with criminals and emergencies.

"I'm glad you enjoy this," she told him. "You know, if you want more Christmassy stuff to do, you could come with Nonna and me when we go get a tree. I'm sure we could use the manpower when it comes to setting the thing up."

"Just give me a day and a time, and I'll be there," he said. "As long as this calm streak at the department keeps up, my schedule is looking pretty clear."

She smiled her thanks and blew on her mug of hot cocoa. It seemed like things were finally settling down in Kittiport, and she couldn't be happier. A nice, calm holiday season was just what they all needed before the new year came in with whatever adventures awaited them.

CHAPTER FOUR

A howling snowstorm ushered in the next week. Ellie decided it was better to be safe than sorry, and shut down all deliveries during the storm. They missed quite a bit of business, but when she saw how many cars there were in the ditch when she drove into work Tuesday morning, she didn't regret her decision in the slightest. The pizzeria could survive a couple of days with fewer sales. Her employees' lives were worth a lot more than the few hundred dollars she would have made if she'd kept deliveries going.

It was still snowing when Papa Pacelli's opened that afternoon, but it had slowed down enough that the plows were able to keep the roads clear, and the entire crew at the pizzeria was kept busy as hungry guests popped in to pick up their orders. Ellie had printed off a large poster reminding everyone of the change in their hours for the next few days, and had also gotten a few hundred flyers advertising their new drive-up window, which she taped to the top of the pizza boxes as they went out. As the time for their early closing and the beginning of construction drew nearer, there was an air of excitement throughout the pizzeria. Everyone was looking forward to the new window. It would make things a lot easier for both her guests and her employees, especially during the cold season.

It would also be a significant move towards one of Ellie's long-term goals; she wanted to begin making the pizzeria's dining area more like a real sit-down restaurant. She planned on expanding the menu throughout the coming year, and with more options on the board such as pasta, salads, and desserts, she hoped they would begin attracting a wider range of people.

Right now, most of her guests picked up their pizza and left; only a handful of people ate inside. With the new pickup window in the back, she could begin making more changes to the dining area, focusing less on keeping an easy path from the door to the register, and more on decorating and creating a comfortable atmosphere.

When three o'clock in the afternoon rolled around, Ellie had Clara turn off the neon sign in the front window and tape a *Closed for Construction* sign on the front door, then she, Clara, and Rose worked together to cover up all of the appliances with sheets of heavy plastic. They spread some old bed sheets across the floor, and made sure the pantry door was tightly shut. The last thing they needed was dust from the construction all over their supplies.

"Thanks for helping," Ellie said when they had finished. "Enjoy the extra time off."

"We will," Rose assured her. "It will be nice to get home when it's still light out for once."

"I'm not scheduled to work until Friday," Clara said. "This is going to be great. I may stop in Thursday evening anyway, though, just to see how it turns out."

"Better yet, order a pizza and pick it up at the new window," Ellie suggested, smiling.

"I will."

The two young women waved goodbye and left through the back door. A gust of wind blew a few flakes of snow in. Ellie was glad that she would get home early today—it was the perfect snowy evening to drink hot cocoa and read a book by the fireplace with Bunny curled up beside her.

The contractor arrived just a few minutes later, stomping off his boots inside the door and giving her hand a firm shake before looking around.

"Glad to see you again, Mr. Bidwell," she said.

"Call me Nathan," he said amiably. "Looks like you're all set, huh? That's good. The men will be here soon, I just wanted to go over things with you one last time before we get started."

They sat down at the round table in the back of the kitchen that the employees used on their breaks. Nathan pulled a folder out of a sleek leather briefcase and withdrew a sketch of the pizzeria's back wall, and the new pickup window.

"Everything look all right?" he asked her.

"It's perfect," she said. "I can't wait to see it in real life."

"You'll be handing pizzas out of it in no time at all," he said with a smile. "I'd like to thank you again for choosing Bidwell Contracting for this project."

"You won me over when you told me that you weren't a fan of Cheesaroni," she told him. "I figured if you don't like them, then you've got to be a good guy."

He laughed as he returned the sketch and the folder to his briefcase. "Well, I'm glad I made an impression. I'm sure you'll be happy with our work. Have a great day, Ms. Pacelli."

As Ellie drove home, she thought back over the last few weeks. She was still in a state of shock over the fact that Papa Pacelli's was hers. She had grown to love the pizzeria, not just as her grandfather's business, but for the warm, welcoming place that it was to so many of Kittiport's citizens. She really hoped that she was doing the right thing by adding this pickup window; now that the process had irrevocably begun, she found that she was having doubts. Would the fact that fewer people would be coming into the pizzeria mean that she would lose some of her chances to develop friendly relationships with her customers? She didn't want to lose that special connection to her guests.

I'll just have to wait and see, she thought with a sigh. *Hopefully my gut was right. At least if this was a mistake, it's not such a big one.* If the pickup window didn't end up working out as well as she planned, it would be easy enough to return to the way they were doing things now.

She took the turn onto her road slowly. It was still snowing, and the roads were caked with half-frozen slush and occasional dangerous patches of ice. The sun was already well down in the sky even though it was still late afternoon, and she knew it would be completely dark in under two hours. *Definitely the perfect sort of day for hot cocoa*, she thought.

The snow began falling even harder the next day, and didn't stop until sometime late Wednesday night. When Ellie opened the back door to let Bunny outside the next morning, she found herself looking out at an unbroken expanse of pure white that reached past the papillon's shoulders. The little dog left a trough through the snow, and needed to be wiped off with a dish towel when she came back inside.

"This sure is beautiful," Ellie said, sparing another glance at the sparkling field of snow between the house and the trees before she shut the back door. "It probably isn't the best day to take another walk, though. You'd have to tunnel through the drifts, wouldn't you, Bunny?"

It was a peaceful, quiet sort of morning; the sort of morning that Ellie would have usually taken the time to enjoy had she not been so eager to see the finished pickup window at the pizzeria later that day. She had called Mr. Bidwell—Nathan, as he wanted to be called—but had yet to hear back from him. She hoped everything was going smoothly; with the amount of snow they had gotten over the past few days, she wouldn't be surprised if some areas had lost power. Ellie decided to assume that no news meant good news, and forced herself to focus on other things while she waited to hear back from the contractor.

The call came just before four that afternoon. Ellie was trying to convince Marlowe to eat some baked sweet potatoes, but the bird wasn't having any of it. When her phone rang, she nearly dropped the dish in her excitement, making Marlowe squawk and jump sideways. She shot a quick apology at the bird as she hurried across the room to grab her phone from the table where it was charging.

She felt a stab of disappointment when she saw that the call wasn't from the contractor, as she had been hoping. Instead, it was Iris. Ellie realized her employees were probably wondering if they were going to be coming in to work at all that day—she had told them she would give them a call when she heard from the contractor that the renovations were finished, but it was already past the time that she had expected to hear from him.

"Hey," she said, answering the phone just before the call went to voicemail. "I'm sorry to keep you waiting, but Mr. Bidwell hasn't called yet, so I still don't know if we'll be able to open today or if there was some sort of delay."

"Ms. P…."

Ellie was surprised to hear the young woman on the other end of the phone choke back a sob. "What's wrong, Iris?" she asked, her heart rate kicking into overdrive.

"The police said to call you… you need to get down here. Jacob and I found him behind the pizzeria. We thought we'd stop by to see how the work was going and we saw him in the snow—"

"Iris, slow down. What's going on?"

"It's the contractor," her employee said. "Ms. Pacelli… he's dead."

CHAPTER FIVE

After Iris hung up, Ellie slid the cellphone into her pocket with shaking fingers and looked blankly down at Bunny, who was sniffing her slippers. Part of her mind insisted that this couldn't be real. She must have misheard Iris. That's right, she would go into town and find out that all of this had been a misunderstanding. Someone had gotten hurt, maybe, but no one would be dead.

Feeling like she was in a dream, Ellie shoved her feet into socks and a pair of boots, grabbed her coat and purse from the counter, and walked out the front door, barely remembering to lock it behind her. She fumbled for a moment at her car as she knocked enough snow off of the door with her bare hands so she could get the key in the lock. After starting the engine, she spent a few desperate moments removing the snow and ice from the windshield, then tossed the scraper on the back seat and used the windshield wipers to clear the rest of the front window.

Even though the interior of her car was toasty warm by the time she pulled into the pizzeria's parking lot, Ellie felt cold. There was an ambulance parked behind the building, along with a pair of patrol cars. Ellie saw her two employees standing by the back entrance, and made a beeline towards them as soon as she parked her car. Liam intercepted her before she reached them.

"The sheriff wants to talk to you," he said without preamble. "He's inside."

Ellie followed him past Jacob and Iris and into the building. With the plastic sheeting over all of the appliances and snow blown in across the floor, the kitchen had a sad, unused look. Russell was flipping through some papers on the table, but looked up when he noticed her and Liam.

"I'll leave you to it," his deputy said. "The coroner will be here in five minutes. The paramedics are on their way out. They called time of death as over twenty-four hours ago, but can't get more exact than that."

"What happened?" Ellie asked once they were alone. "How could something like this—"

"We're still trying to figure all of that out," Russell said. "I only got the call about twenty minutes ago. When I heard a body had been found at Papa Pacelli's, my first thought was that it was you. You have no idea how relieved I was when I learned the victim was a man. I don't think I've ever felt relief in relation to a murder before."

"Someone murdered him?" she said, her eyes going wide. "You're sure?"

The sheriff nodded. "The murder weapon was found just feet away from his body. One of your employees found it, in fact."

"Oh my goodness," Ellie breathed. "Which one?"

"The young woman with the colored hair, the new one… I wrote her name down—" He flipped through the small, pocket sized notebook that he kept in his jacket pocket.

"That's Iris," Ellie said. "The poor girl. How much longer do you need to keep her here?"

"She's already agreed to come down to the station with Bethany," Russell said. "Since she touched the murder weapon, we need to record her fingerprints. Your other employee will be free to go once Liam's done talking to him. I'll need to ask you some questions too, but first I wanted to make sure you're okay."

"I'm still in shock," she admitted. "I saw him yesterday. He was so nice. I can't believe he's dead. He didn't deserve that."

"They never do," the sheriff said grimly. "But we'll do everything we can to catch the person who killed him. Now, I need to ask you a few questions, if you're feeling up to it."

"Of course," Ellie said. "Anything I can do to help."

"Here, we can sit down." He pulled out a chair, and she gingerly sat in it. He seemed to realize what she was thinking. "Don't worry about contaminating any evidence. The back door was locked when we arrived, and there are no signs that anything in here has been disturbed. I don't believe the killer came inside at all."

"Do you think it might have been a random attack? A mugging, maybe?"

"It's hard to say." He sat down across from her and got ready to take notes. "Are you ready to begin?"

The questioning session didn't take long, since Ellie couldn't answer most of Russell's questions, but she helped where she could. Some of the shock started wearing off, and she found herself faced with a problem that was minor in the face of a man's murder, but had a serious impact on the pizzeria. What in the world was she going to do with a gaping hole in the back of her kitchen?

The construction crew had only gotten as far as cutting a rough hole in the wall, and draping plastic sheeting over it to protect the kitchen from the elements while they were gone. To Ellie, it didn't look as if they had spent more than a few hours in total on the project. She wasn't sure what came next; would she have to find a new contractor? How long would it take to untangle the mess that Nathan Bidwell's murder had left behind?

Once she had answered everything that she could, Russell told her that she and Jacob were free to go. They wouldn't be able to open the pizzeria at all that day, which she had expected. Still, it was an additional blow on top of everything else. The weather was warming up, the roads were clear for the first time in days; in other words, this was likely to be a busy day in Kittiport as people ventured out after the snowstorm.

"Hey, Ms. P," Jacob said, taking a hand out of his jacket pocket to give her a subdued wave when he saw her leave the pizzeria.

"Hi, Jacob," she said, walking over to where he was leaning against the back of the pizzeria. "Are you still waiting to be questioned?"

"Nah, Deputy Lafferre said I was free to go. I was just waiting for you."

"Sorry, I don't have any answers for you. You probably know more than I do at this point. All I know is that Mr. Bidwell is dead, and you and Iris found him."

"Iris is the one that found him, actually. I didn't even get out of the car until I saw her drop the hammer and stumble backwards. We just stopped by to see how things were looking, then we were going to carpool to the community college, since we've both got some final exams to finish up before Christmas break."

"She dropped a hammer?" Ellie asked, utterly confused.

"She picked up a hammer from the ground," he said. "I guess the police think it was the murder weapon or something. You should ask her about it, she's better at explaining things than I am."

"I don't want to make her talk about it until she's ready," Ellie said. "I'm sure she's already explained everything to the police a couple of times. Did she leave already/"

"Yeah, she went to the sheriff's department with one of the deputies. I don't think she'll mind talking about it. She said she wanted to see you when she was done having her fingerprints recorded."

Ellie and Jacob drove their cars over to the sheriff's department and waited inside for Iris. It wasn't long before the young woman with the brightly colored hair appeared and announced that she was free to go. Ellie offered to pay for a late lunch, and the two young adults took her up on the offer gratefully.

They ended up at a small café that served sandwiches and soups in addition to fresh pastries and, of course, steaming mugs of coffee and cocoa. The pizzeria owner told them she was treating, and within minutes the three of them were seated at a small table in the corner with their food and drinks in front of them. They ate in silence for a moment while Ellie tried to figure out where to start.

"I'm sorry you two had to be there and see that," she said at last. "I feel like it was my fault, somehow…"

"It's not like you killed the guy," Iris said. "We're the ones that decided to stop by and see how the construction was coming. Plus, it's better that we found him than someone else. What if some kid decided to cut through the parking lot after school or something?"

"I still feel bad. I know how horrible it is to see a body."

"It was more surprising than anything. I didn't even realize what I was seeing at first. He was partially covered by snow." Iris frowned, poking at her bread bowl with a spoon. "I just can't stop thinking about his family. That's what really gets me. Do you know if he had kids or anything?"

"I don't," Ellie said. She didn't even want to imagine what his next of kin must be going through right now. She didn't envy whoever it was that had to make that call. "If you don't mind talking about it, would it be all right if I asked you to tell me everything that happened? I know that you told all of this to the police already. Don't worry about it if you don't want to talk about it again."

"Nah, that's fine. There isn't much to tell. Jacob texted me a few hours ago to ask if I had heard from you, and I hadn't, so we decided to wait for another hour or two and then go see how things were going with the construction crew. If it looked like they were almost done, we'd stick around, but if it looked like they still had a lot to do, we decided we would call you and then head out to the community college to take our finals while the roads are clear." She took a sip of her soda, then continued. "Anyway, when we got there, the parking lot was empty, and there were no fresh tracks in the snow. I couldn't tell how much progress they had made, so I got out of the car to take a look under the plastic they put up to cover the window hole. When I got closer to the building, I saw a hammer sticking out of the snow by the door. I thought one of the guys must have dropped it, so I picked it up… then I saw Mr. Bidwell leaning against the building. He was covered in snow, so I knew right away he was dead."

Ellie thanked her employee for telling her story. Her mind was racing. Liam had told Russell that the paramedics thought Nathan Bidwell had been dead for at least a day. How had no one noticed he was missing? What about the men who he had hired to work on the window? She was surprised that none of them had shown up to work the day before. They would have found his body immediately, of course. What was going on here? Who had killed Mr. Bidwell, and why?

CHAPTER SIX

With the pizzeria closed for another day while the police investigated the crime scene, Ellie decided to try to accomplish at least one of the tasks on her to-do list. Christmas tree shopping was something she hadn't done for years. It hadn't been realistic to haul a real tree up to her apartment every year back when she lived in Chicago, so she had made do with a fake one from the craft store.

Now she was in the Pacelli house instead of a small apartment, and the high ceiling in the living room was just begging for a splendid pine tree. She had been looking forward to Russell accompanying them to get the tree, but that was out of the question now that he had another murder to solve. The thought of leaving him behind made her feel guilty, but there wasn't anything she could do. If it was possible for her to help investigate alongside him, she would do that in a heartbeat. She knew he wouldn't like that idea, though, so she would just have to do what she *could* do, and that meant getting a Christmas tree with her grandmother.

Marcel's Tree Farm was only a couple of miles out of town. The weather was even nicer than it had been the day before, and in what might be the last warm day of the year, the snow was beginning to melt. The roads were clear and mostly dry, and Nonna was in an unusually good mood.

"Ooh, I haven't been out here in *ages*," she said. "I used to love stopping at that little convenience shop on the corner with your grandfather. They sell everything in there."

"It looked closed," Ellie said. "But if it's still open, we can stop on the way back, if you want."

The tree farm was busy; Ellie guessed that people were taking advantage of the nice weather and getting their tree before it turned freezing again. She didn't blame them—it was nice not to have to wear gloves and a winter coat just to stay comfortable.

A young woman who looked young enough to be in high school approached them as they got out of the car. "Hi! My name is Miranda. Do you guys know what kind of tree you're looking for today?"

Ellie looked towards her grandmother, who nodded firmly and said, "Yes. I always get white pine."

"The white pines will be down that path and to the right," the young woman said. "You can recognize employees by our red and green striped hats. Any one of us will be happy to assist you in cutting down and loading up your tree. Any of the trees available in areas marked with silver tinsel are available for sale."

Ellie offered her arm to Nonna, and the two of them set off down the path, picking their way carefully around patches of slushy mud. It wasn't long before they found themselves in a field of small white pines, varying in size from about four feet tall to well over their heads.

"What size should we get?" Ellie asked. "Do you think it would be best to get something small, since it will probably be only the two of us?" She wanted a huge tree, but it was her grandmother's house and she didn't know how much the older woman would appreciate the mess and needles from a large tree.

"Didn't I tell you?" Nonna asked. "Your father responded to my email. He says he might stop by on Christmas Eve for the family dinner."

"Dad?" The pizzeria owner blinked. She hadn't seen her father in twenty years. They had sent emails back and forth occasionally, but she had always gotten the feeling that she was a part of his life that he would rather put behind him.

"He didn't seem very certain in his email," her grandmother said. "But you know how it goes… he might show up, he might not. I want everything to be perfect just in case he does."

"Right, we'll get a big tree, then," Ellie said. "One as big as we can fit in the living room."

After twenty damp minutes, she and Nonna agreed that they had found the perfect tree. It was tall and full with a straight trunk, and in Ellie's opinion was everything a Christmas tree should be. She ran her fingers across the long, soft needles. They were just as she remembered from all of the Christmases she had spent at her grandmother's house as a child, so unlike the short, sharp needles that fell from the trees her mother had always chosen.

"We'll take this one," she told the first tree farm employee she saw.

Before long, the tree had been cut down, shaken, and bundled up on top of her car. It looked huge on top of the vehicle, and Ellie hoped it would make the trip home without falling off. She tested one of the ropes gingerly. It *seemed* to be tied on well enough. She would just have to remember to take the turns slowly. It was beginning to dawn on her that she was going to have quite the job getting it in the house on her own.

She remembered her promise to her grandmother just as the small corner store came into view. She slowed down carefully and turned into the empty lot. She pulled up close enough to the building to read the sign on the window. *We moved! New Location is Located at the Corner of Barton St. and Marsh St.*

"I'm sorry," she said to the older woman. "Do you want to go find the new shop?"

"It's all right." Nonna sighed. "I had such good memories there with your grandfather. It won't be the same in a new building."

Ellie gazed at the *For Sale* sign for a moment before pulling away from the building. With how well things had been going at the pizzeria lately—not counting the murder—it was easy to think about expanding the restaurant. She didn't want to get ahead of herself, though. Maybe one day she would open a second pizzeria, but right now it would be best for her to focus on what she already had.

They got back to the Pacelli house with the tree still firmly attached to the roof of the car and none the worse for the trip. Ellie helped Nonna inside, then began the task of making room for the tree in the corner of the living room by the fireplace. She had already brought the stand and the tree skirt up from the basement, so all that was left to do was move an end table and a lamp out of the way, and lock Bunny in the office so the little dog wouldn't try to escape while she was wrestling the tree in through the door.

Armed with a pair of gloves and a knife to cut the ropes, she propped the front door open and went out to the car. After a few minutes spent hacking through the knots, she pulled the tree down from the car and stood it up. So far so good.

After a few attempts to carry it, she ended up dragging the tree up to the front steps and through the door. With the netting still on, it was an easy enough fit. The most difficult part was getting it to stand up straight in the stand. With Nonna's help, they managed eventually, and at long last it was time to cut through the net and admire the tree in its full glory.

"It fits in here perfectly," Ellie said. "Though we might need to take a bit off the top for the star."

"I don't know, it might fit," Nonna said. "Do you want me to make hot cocoa before we get started on the decorations?"

Over the next few hours, Ellie was almost able to forget about Nathan's murder. With hot cocoa, Christmas music, and the sharp pine scent of the tree they were decorating, it was hard to think of anything but the coming holiday. She felt happy, but also felt guilty about her happiness. A man was dead, and here she was, singing along to "Jingle Bells" and standing on tiptoe to put an ornament on one of the higher branches.

He won't ever get to do any of these things again. That thought sobered her. It was too late to save Nathan Bidwell, but she would do everything in her power to help him get justice.

Feeling less cheery, but more determined, Ellie forced her focus back on the task at hand. She didn't know how many more

Christmases she was going to have with her grandmother, and she wanted to make the most of every second while she could.

CHAPTER SEVEN

"What are you going to do about the pizzeria renovation?" Shannon Ward asked as she pulled out of her friend's driveway.

Ellie, who was digging through her purse to make sure she had all of her coupons, sighed. "I don't know. It doesn't feel right to hire someone else so soon after the original contractor was killed, but at the same time, I can't ask my employees to work in a freezing kitchen for weeks. That plastic keeps the snow out, but it doesn't work for insulation. We really need the new window to be installed as soon as possible."

The pizzeria was opening later that morning for the first time since Tuesday, and Ellie knew it would not be a fun day. The combination of it being a Saturday, and the restaurant having been closed for so long meant that they were bound to be busy. The kitchen was sure to be freezing even with all of the ovens running. She had considered bringing a space heater with her when she went in for opening, but there wasn't anywhere to put one where it wouldn't be a tripping hazard. They would just have to make do for now, but the sooner the window was installed, the better.

"I can ask James if he can handle it," Shannon suggested.

"No, no, don't bother him with that," Ellie said. "I'm sure he's got a lot of other things on his plate."

"I don't think he'd mind. He'd probably even do it for free. I mean, you're my best friend and you're dating his brother. You're practically family."

That was exactly what she did not want. Mixing business with Russell's family didn't seem like a good idea. She had seen firsthand how easily things could implode when you mixed your business and personal life. She didn't want to make that mistake again.

"I think I've already got someone in mind," she told her friend. "I really don't want to ask James for anything else. He's always been so nice to me, even after all of the crazy stuff I've dragged you into."

Shannon snorted. "What do you mean 'dragged me into'? I was a fully willing participant in our adventures, thanks very much. Speaking of crazy stuff… have you spoken to Karen recently?"

"Not within the past week, no. Why?"

"I was just wondering if she heard about what happened to that poor man. She already thinks the two of us are trouble magnets. I wouldn't be surprised if this scared her away for good."

Karen was a psychologist that worked in Benton Harbor, a small town down the coast from Kittiport. She had begun a cautious friendship with Ellie and Shannon after the three of them had been held in a room together by a crazed murderer. Being held at knifepoint had proven a unique bonding experience, and the three of them had gotten together for lunch once or twice a week since.

"I'm sure she'll read about it in the paper sooner or later," the pizzeria owner said. She sighed. "I suppose she should hear it from me first. I just know she's going to freak out. It's nice that she cares, but she must realize I don't get involved in this stuff on *purpose.* Telling me to be careful won't help. I'm *already* careful."

"I'm not sure if careful is the right word to describe you," Shannon smiled. "Where's that pepper spray Russell bought you?"

"On top of my dresser," Ellie admitted. "I put it there when I switched purses, and forgot to start carrying it again. But that doesn't mean I'm not careful… I just haven't got into the habit of carrying it with me yet. Plus, who's going to have time to dig around in their purse if they're getting attacked?"

"I think you're supposed to put it on your key chain," her friend said. "Anyway, we should probably decide where we're going first. Who are you shopping for today?"

"I need to get something for my grandmother. That's the priority right now. She's done so much for me, and Christmas is the perfect opportunity to show her how much I appreciate everything. If we have time, I'd like to get a small gift for each of my employees as well, plus something for Russell."

"Russ is on my list, too. He should be easy enough to shop for if we can find a fishing store. I need to find something for James, as well as some of the gals at the paper. Do you want to start by looking around some of the antique shops? You might find something for your nonna there, and I'm sure I can find some things my coworkers would like."

"Sure, sounds like a plan."

Christmas shopping in northern Maine was a far cry from Christmas shopping in Chicago. Ellie trusted Shannon to know where all of the good shops and hidden gems were in the neighboring towns. With only a few hours until she had to get to the pizzeria, they didn't have long, but if she could find the perfect gift for even one person on her list, she would be happy.

The first antique shop they stopped at was tiny and dark, with case after case of expensive-looking jewelry. A mink coat was hanging on a stand near the register. Ellie looked at the price tag and winced.

"They don't make fur like this anymore," said a voice. She and Shannon both jumped. Sitting in a chair against the wall was an older man that neither of them had noticed.

"Can I help you ladies with anything?" he asked, rising slowly with the aid of a cane. "A necklace for a mother, perhaps?"

"I'm looking for something for my grandmother," Ellie said. "She doesn't really wear much jewelry, besides her wedding ring."

"Well, take your time looking around. If you'd like to see something in one of the cases, let me know. I have to go get the keys from the back room."

"All right," she told the man. "Thanks."

She and Shannon walked around the dimly lit store, talking in whispers as they pointed out neat pieces of jewelry to each other. Ellie wasn't sure what exactly she was looking for, but was certain she would know it when she found it. She wanted to get a truly special present for her grandmother. She owed the woman so much, it seemed almost impossible to find something that would express her gratitude.

"This is where James got my engagement ring," Shannon told her in a low voice. "He knew how much I love old items with stories, so he thought I would appreciate something from here more than a brand-new ring. He was right, of course."

"You two are so lucky to have each other," Ellie whispered back. "Not many people are as happy as the two of you are, especially not after they've been married to their high school sweetheart for almost twenty years."

"He's a special guy," her friend agreed. "And the love of my life."

Ellie felt a surge of envy towards her best friend. She would love to have a relationship as good as Shannon's was with James. Someone to grow old with, someone to depend on when things got rough, someone to share all of her happiest moments with…

"What about this?" Shannon asked, startling her out of her thoughts.

"What?"

"Right there, next to that bracelet. Do you think your grandmother might like it? I know you said she doesn't really wear much jewelry, but this could have personal meaning to her. Like her wedding ring."

"You're right." Ellie gazed into the glass case for a long moment. "Shannon, I think you've found the perfect gift for Nonna."

With only one person crossed off their list, Shannon and Ellie made their way to the next antique shop after Ellie purchased the gift for her grandmother. There was still more that she had to do to complete it, but she felt better knowing that the puzzle of what to get the older woman had been solved.

As they shopped, they talked. Even though both women got to make their own schedules, for the most part, they were usually both too busy, so it was rare for them to be able to spend this much time together without one of them having to run off to do something.

"What are your Christmas plans?" Shannon asked as they strolled down the fishing aisle of a sports store together. They were looking for something for Russell now, which was easier said than done since Ellie knew next to nothing about fishing. She had a date with him the next night, and could ask him if there was anything he wanted then, but would prefer his gift to be a surprise.

"Nonna and I are going to have dinner together on Christmas Eve. My father might join us. On Christmas Day, I don't think we're going to do much besides exchange gifts and take a well-deserved break."

"Your father?" her friend asked. "You haven't seen him for what, over twenty years?"

"Right. I saw him once after the divorce, and that's it. The last time I saw him, he would have been around my age."

"Wow," Shannon said. "It's going to be interesting if he comes. I hope he does, it would be nice for the two of you to catch up."

"Do you have any plans for Christmas, or are you and James just staying around the house and doing your own thing?" Ellie asked, changing the subject as smoothly as she could.

"My sister Sara is coming over," her friend said. "Do you remember her? She's two years younger than us. We didn't really get along when we were younger, so you might not have seen her much. Russell will be coming over on Christmas too, unless he finds some excuse to work."

"I'm sure seeing her will bring something back, though I can't really say that I remember anything about her offhand," Ellie said. "Now what in the world should I get your brother-in-law?"

CHAPTER EIGHT

They managed to find gifts for Russell while they were out, but by the time they had paid for their purchases and walked back to the car, it was time for Ellie to head to work.

As she splashed through the slush in the parking lot, she tried not to look too closely at the spot where Nathan's body had been found. It didn't feel right to pretend that nothing had happened and proceed with business as usual, but she didn't know what else to do. She would never understand how someone could so casually and cruelly take another person's life. It made her sick to think about, so she focused instead on getting the pizzeria up and running again.

Inside the kitchen, it wasn't as cold as she had feared it would be. Of course, it was warmer out today than it would be for most of the week; they were due for another cold front to roll in this evening, and this one looked like it would be there to stay.

The plastic in the kitchen had protected the appliances, and it was easy enough to mop up the floor, but after days of being closed, a light coat of dust covered the tables and booths in the dining area. Armed with a rag and a bottle of cleaner, Ellie scrubbed the room from top to bottom. She didn't want to give any of her guests a reason to avoid the pizzeria; by now, it would already be well known that a man had been killed on the premises. She could only hope that not too many of her customers were scared away by that.

With the cleaning finished and a good hour to go before it was time to open, the pizzeria owner decided to put together a new pizza of the week to give her customers something to stop in and try. She enjoyed doing seasonal pizzas, but was stumped by what to put on a pizza for Christmas. There weren't any veggies that were in season in winter in Maine. *It's not like I can put mistletoe on a gingerbread crust and call it a pizza*, she thought. *Actually, a gingerbread crust sounds good. Maybe I could do some sort of special holiday dessert pizza.* She shook her head, trying not to get distracted. She needed to come up with some sort of holiday-themed pizza before Papa Pacelli's opened. It was time to experiment.

"It smells great in here," Rose said as she pushed in through the employee entrance forty-five minutes later. "What is that?"

"It's a ham, fig, and ricotta thin-crust pizza," Ellie told her. "I just pulled it out of the oven. I thought it could be our special for the coming week. We need something to boost people's spirits after the murder."

"Figs on a pizza?" the young woman asked doubtfully as she pulled off her coat and hung her purse on a hook.

"I think it will be good." The pizzeria owner gave the pizza a critical look. It *smelled* good, at least. She hadn't tried it yet; one of the things she had learned from working at Papa Pacelli's over the past few months was that it was smart to wait for the pizza to cool for a few minutes before grabbing a slice. Pizza sauce right out of the oven was *hot,* and she had suffered the dreaded 'pizza mouth'—burns to the roof of her mouth—too many times to make that mistake again any time soon.

"Is this one for us?"

"Yeah, I thought the three of us could eat it for lunch. If it's any good, we can put it on the menu."

"Awesome, I'll cut it if you want. Then we can all eat when Iris gets here."

Ellie took the first cautious bite once they were all seated around the table in the kitchen. She wasn't sure what to expect from her ad-libbed holiday pizza, but was pleasantly surprised by the results. The saltiness of the ham offset the sweetness of the fig, and the ricotta pulled everything together just perfectly. She thought it would be good cold, too, which wasn't something she could say about all pizzas.

"What do you think?" she asked her employees.

"I like it," Rose said. "It's different, but it's good. Are we going to do a holiday calzone, too?"

"Feel free to experiment if you'd like to," Ellie told her. The calzones were a relatively new addition to the pizzeria, and were a steady seller. She doubted Jeffrey and Xavier would ever forgive her for stealing away their signature dish, but as far as she was concerned, that was no loss. The two of them had caused enough problems for her. She didn't have any desire to play nice any more.

"What do you think, Iris?" Rose asked.

"Hmm? Oh, it's good." The young woman looked down at her pizza, which only had one bite taken out of it. She had been unusually quiet since she had gotten there. Usually, she was full of energy from the moment she stepped foot inside the building.

"Is everything all right?" Ellie asked her, concerned.

"Yeah, I'm fine." Her employee forced a smile. "The pizza is good, I'm just not very hungry right now. I'll put my piece in the fridge and eat it later. You guys can finish the rest, if you want."

The pizzeria owner watched as the young woman walked away. Something was definitely going on with her, but she wasn't going to push the matter. She caught Rose's eye, and saw that the other girl looked puzzled too. What was going on with Iris?

The sound of a car door slamming shut in the parking lot behind the deli tore her away from her thoughts. They had work to do; trying to figure out how to help her employee cope with the murder would just have to wait.

"I'm going to go unlock the door and turn the sign on," Ellie announced. "Will the two of you finish up in here? I have a feeling we're going to be busy today."

A steady stream of customers walked through their doors from the time they opened well into the evening. A few of them seemed more interested in hearing about the murder than buying food. Luckily, Rose didn't seem to mind telling the story when they asked. Iris, on the other hand, was much more reluctant to speak of it. Ellie wondered what had happened—the young woman hadn't seemed to mind talking about it with her and Jacob later the same day that Nathan Bidwell had been killed. She hoped Iris was coping all right with everything that had happened, but she didn't feel like she knew the new employee well enough to ask.

By the time it started getting dark out and the temperature began to fall, she decided that enough was enough. She needed to hire someone else to finish installing the new window. The longer she waited, the colder and more miserable it was going to get. Sometimes practicality had to take precedence, and although she still felt uncomfortable with replacing Nathan within days of his death, she was even more uncomfortable with asking her employees to work with a gaping hole in the wall.

It didn't take long for her to pull up the number for another contractor. She decided to go with the man who had given her the lowest bid. All that was left to do was to touch up the hole and install the window; she figured it would be hard to mess up even for someone who had only mediocre reviews.

He answered on the second ring and immediately agreed to take the job. "We can start as soon as Monday," he told her.

"Perfect. We're going to be freezing our fingers off in here, so the sooner the better."

"When do you want my men there? We can come out at night, after you're closed."

"That would be wonderful," she told him. "I don't want to have to cut back our hours any more if we don't have to."

With the issue of the window settled, Ellie felt as if a weight had been lifted from her shoulders. She was beginning to get things gradually under control again. She had made a dent in her Christmas shopping list, and she had made arrangements to have the drive-through window installed. It wasn't much, but it was a start. If only she could make some progress in figuring out who had killed Nathan Bidwell. She didn't think anyone in town would be able to completely relax until his killer was safely behind bars.

CHAPTER NINE

The White Pine Kitchen was the nicest restaurant in town, and the go-to spot for special occasions for everyone in Kittiport. Ellie enjoyed going there on dates with Russell. It gave her a chance to dress up, and the food was always phenomenal. There had been only one occasion where she had experienced poor service there, and at the time half the town had thought she was a murderer, so she didn't hold a grudge for that.

Sunday evenings were always a busy time at the Kitchen, but Russell had called ahead to reserve a table for them, so their wait was only a few minutes long. With the pizzeria closed for the evening, Ellie didn't expect any interruptions. Of course, the sheriff was on call as always, but unless there was a break in the murder case, chances were they wouldn't be interrupted.

"This place is really done up for the holidays," she said as they took their seats. She was always one to admire Christmas decorations, and the White Pine Kitchen gave her a lot to admire.

"It's almost as festive as the pizzeria," Russell said, the corner of his mouth quirking up in a grin.

"I know, I know, I'm one to talk," she said, laughing. "I really like what they did, though. The soft white lights are so much more subtle and soft than the colored ones. Do you think Papa Pacelli's is over the top?"

"No, it's just perfect for the sort of restaurant it is," he said. "A family-friendly pizza place."

"I hope so… I *have* had a few people tell me how much they like it. It's going to look so plain when I take all of the decorations down after the holiday."

"It will be fine," he assured her. "I'm sure most of your customers stop by for the food, anyway, not the atmosphere."

"You're probably right," she said. "Ever since Nonna gave me the pizzeria, I've just felt such a huge responsibility to do well. I know how much it means to her."

"You're doing fine," he said. "I think you worry about the wrong things."

"What do you mean?" she asked.

"Well, you do have sort of a habit of getting in over your head." When she raised her eyebrows, he added, "You recently got kidnapped by a murderer and fell off a roof, Ellie. But you're focused on whether your customers like your interior decorating."

"I didn't get kidnapped," she said, somewhat miffed. "I went with him perfectly willingly. And I didn't know he was a killer at the time."

Russell chuckled and shook his head. "Telling me you went with a killer willingly isn't going to help me stop worrying about you." He grew more serious. "Especially now that another crime has occurred in connection with Papa Pacelli's. Do you have your pepper spray with you?"

"I forgot to put it in my new purse," she admitted. "Shannon suggested that I keep it on my key chain, so I'll try to do that when I get home."

They paused in their conversation while their waiter took their drink order. When they were alone again, Ellie brought up a different subject.

"So, have you had any breaks in the case?" she asked.

"I hate to say it, but no," the sheriff said. He frowned. "If we just had something to go on… the problem is that there was very little in the way of evidence left at the crime scene. There were no fingerprints on the murder weapon besides those belonging to the victim, and of course your employee, Iris. We determined that the hammer belonged to the victim, and of course Iris was the one who found the hammer, so there's no surprise there."

"Do you think that the fact that there were no other fingerprints means the murder was premeditated? The killer might have put on gloves before attacking Nathan or something."

"If it wasn't winter, I would agree with you," he said. "But the day that the murder happened was cold, and most people were probably wearing gloves. We don't have any evidence one way or the other whether the murder was planned or random."

"Were there footprints or tire tracks that you could follow?" she asked.

"Anything left behind by the killer would have been covered with snow, and then obliterated when the emergency vehicles showed up," he told her. "Good thinking, though."

"I know you have probably gone through all of this with your deputies," she said. "Sorry, it's probably not what you wanted to talk about on a date. It's just hard not to feel like I should try to help. If it wasn't for me, he would still be alive right now."

"How do you figure that?" he asked, raising an eyebrow.

"Well, I'm the one who hired him. If I had gone with another contractor, then he wouldn't have been killed."

"Someone else may have been, though," Russell said. "If it was a random killing, like a mugging, then it could have happened to anyone you had hired. If someone was targeting Nathan specifically, then he would have been attacked whether you hired him or not. Don't blame yourself for this. There's no telling how things may have turned out, and no use wondering about it. What happened, happened, and we'll do our best to catch the person responsible and make sure it doesn't happen to anyone else."

Ellie wondered if Russell took his own advice when it came to his wife's death. She didn't know much about it, and couldn't bring herself to ask him. Maybe she would broach the subject with Shannon eventually.

"I still feel like I should be doing something to help solve the murder," she said. "Is there any way I can help?"

"No," he said firmly. "I want you to stay far away from this, Ellie. This person's dangerous. You shouldn't get involved."

"What if he's a customer?" she said. "I could help by asking people questions when they come in, and see if they act suspiciously."

"It's not a good idea, Ellie," he said. "I couldn't stand it if you were this killer's next victim." He reached across the table and took her hand. "Please, just promise me that you won't get involved."

She took a deep breath and looked down at their hands. He cared for her; how could she say no?

“All right,” she said slowly. “I won’t get involved.”

CHAPTER TEN

Monday was a cold but beautiful day. It snowed on and off, and between snowfalls, the sun peeked out. The light, powdery snow began to stick early in the morning, and by the time Ellie got to the pizzeria, the town was wearing a covering of fresh, pure white.

As she turned on the ovens, rolled out the first batches of dough, and chopped fresh vegetables, she thought back on her conversation with Russell during their date the evening before. She knew that she had no business getting involved with something like a murder case. More likely than not, she would just mess it up and get in the way of the men and women who actually knew what they were doing. Still, she couldn't shake the feeling that she should be doing *something* to help. The murder had happened at her restaurant, after all, and only a few weeks after she had officially taken possession of it.

Could Nathan's death have been related to my taking over the restaurant somehow? she wondered. *No, I'm just being ridiculous.* Who would care enough about the little pizzeria to kill someone when it changed hands? Unbidden, the thought of Jeffrey and Xavier from Cheesaroni Calzones popped into her mind.

They may be jerks, but they wouldn't kill someone, she told herself. *And they definitely wouldn't kill Nathan. He was an independent contractor, and hardly even affiliated with the pizzeria. His death probably isn't even connected with Papa Pacelli's at all.*

Of course, that still didn't answer the question of who had killed him, and why. Ellie didn't think it was a random mugging due to the simple fact that nothing had been stolen from the pizzeria. Someone who had committed the crime for money would easily have been able to slip through the hole where the window was going. There were plenty of appliances in the kitchen that someone in desperate need of cash could sell—they weren't top of the line, no, but still worth a pretty penny. Not to mention the fact that anyone willing to put just a little bit of effort forth would have been able to break into the cash register… or just steal the entire thing if it came down to that. She was under no illusions about the level of security in Papa Pacelli's; a ten-year-old could probably rob the place and get cleanly away. But Kittiport was, or had been, a very safe town. Despite the spate of murders since she'd moved there, she didn't see the need for an elaborate security system.

If the murder wasn't connected to the pizzeria, and wasn't random, that meant that someone had a grudge against Nathan specifically. If only she knew more about him… maybe she could do some research on the internet. Of course, if he owed someone money or was involved in some sort of affair, it probably wouldn't show up online.

"I'm sure Russell has already got all of this covered," she said aloud as she began mixing the next batch of dough. She needed to keep her mind on her work. She had already promised the sheriff that she wouldn't get involved, and that was a promise that she intended to keep.

Ellie stayed at the pizzeria for the entire day, from before opening to past closing. The new contractor pulled into the parking lot twenty minutes after she had shut off the sign and locked the front doors. He was late. Normally she wouldn't have minded, but it had been a long day and she was cold and tired, and aching to go home and take a bath.

"How long do you think it will take you?" she asked him after he finished examining the work the original team had already done to the wall.

"My guys can probably finish smoothing out the hole for the window tonight or tomorrow night," he said. "Do you have the window here?"

She nodded. "It was a special order. It's in the storage closet, I'll show you."

He followed her back through the pizzeria and gave the pickup window a once over. "Right, we'll double-check the measurements, but it shouldn't take long to finish the project. We'll have the window in by Wednesday."

Ellie thanked him and left, hoping she had made the right decision by going with the less expensive company. *It's probably going to be fine*, she thought. *They just need to smooth out a few rough edges and install a window. How hard can it be?*

Dinner at the Pacelli house that night was nothing special; reheated pizza leftover from lunch at Papa Pacelli's, and a hastily thrown together salad, with Ellie's first attempt at a gingerbread cookie pie for dessert. They turned Christmas music on softly in the background, and made hot cocoa when they were done.

"Wednesday I'll take you to see the new pickup window," Ellie told her grandmother as they cleaned up after the meal. "It will be nice to have it installed at last. I hope people use it."

"I'm sure they will," the older woman said. "No one wants to walk through the snow if they can help it. I'm glad the project is moving forward. Have you heard anything more about that poor man's death yet?"

"No," Ellie said. "I don't think the police have made any progress on the case. It's not their fault, of course; Russell's doing everything he can to solve it."

"Of course he is," Nonna said. "He's a good man, and I think he's good for you. You could do a lot worse than the sheriff of Kittiport."

"We've only gone on a few dates, Nonna," she said. "We're really just friends."

"Nonsense, I've seen the way he looks at you. There's definitely romance in the air."

"Don't be silly, neither of us have time for romance right now."

"You can't schedule falling in love, dear." With that, the older woman pushed herself to her feet and bid her granddaughter goodnight, leaving Ellie alone in the kitchen to finish the dishes and think back on their conversation.

"She doesn't know what she's talking about," she said softly to Bunny as she finished drying the last of the plates. "It's been decades since she dated. If it makes her feel better to think I'm beginning some storybook romance, I might as well let her. There's no harm in letting her believe something that makes her happy, at least for a little while."

She shut off the kitchen light, grabbed her purse and most recent acquisition from the library, and went upstairs.

An insistent buzzing sound pulled her out of her novel half an hour later. Putting a finger between the pages to hold her spot, Ellie looked around her room until her eyes landed on her purse. She must have forgotten to turn her ringtone back up after leaving the pizzeria.

Wondering who it could be, she walked over to the dresser and pulled the cellphone out. The number on the screen looked familiar, but whoever it was wasn't in her address book. Curious, she answered it.

"Hello?"

"Am I speaking with Ms. Pacelli?"

"Yes, may I ask who's calling?"

"Edward Blatt," came the reply.

Mr. Blatt was the new contractor; she must have forgotten to put his number in her phone.

"Oh." She glanced at her clock. It was getting late. "How is the progress on the window coming?"

"I quit."

"What?"

"I quit the contract. I'm done. I'm not going back there. I don't know what kind of crazy operation you're running, but I don't want a part of it."

Ellie blinked, trying to figure out what she was hearing.

"I don't understand, Mr. Blatt," she said at last. "What happened? What do you mean you quit?"

"After my men left for the night, I was inside cleaning up some of the mess from the drywall, and I heard someone walking around outside. I thought it was one of the guys, coming back to pick up something he had for gotten. I could hear the footsteps get closer and closer to the building, stop, then walk away. I thought it was odd, but didn't pay it no mind. Then when I went outside to leave for the night, I found a bunch of flowers right outside the door. It was creepy, let me tell you, but that wasn't the worst. While I was staring at the flowers, someone came up behind me and tried to hit me on the head! I took off and didn't look back. I'm done, you can find someone else to put that window in for you. I'll send you an invoice for the work we already did."

With that, he hung up. The pizzeria owner starred at her phone, still trying to work through the man's story. What in the world was going on? There was only one person she could think of that would be able to get her any answers. As Ellie dialed Russell's number, her eyes fell on the container of pepper spray on top of the dresser. While she was waiting for him to answer, she installed it on her key chain. If there was some psycho out there with a penchant for hitting people on the head, she didn't want to meet him unprepared.

CHAPTER ELEVEN

Ellie met Russell in the parking lot of the sheriff's department twenty minutes later. He hadn't wanted her to come along, but she had insisted. The pizzeria was her responsibility, after all. She couldn't very well stay at home and read while Russell did all the legwork.

"Liam already checked the scene, and said he didn't find anyone on the premises," he said when she slid into his truck's passenger seat. "He confirms that there is a bouquet of flowers by the rear entrance. He hasn't touched anything in hopes that you would be able to tell us if something was out of place."

"I'll do what I can. Do you think whoever attacked Mr. Blatt might have broken into the pizzeria?"

"Liam said it didn't look like a break-in, but you'll have to give the final word on whether anything was taken or not. Are you ready to go? You have your keys?"

She held up her key chain. "Pepper spray included."

"That's progress." He gave her a tired smile, then pulled out of the parking lot.

Ellie had an eerie sense of déjà vu when Russell parked the truck in the pizzeria's parking lot. She was reminded strongly of the scene from the week before, when Nathan Bidwell's body had been found. The flowers were in the exact same spot, and just like the other day, Liam was waiting for her just outside of the building.

"Careful," he said, putting a hand out to stop them as she and Russell drew near. "Don't step through these two sets of footprints. One of the tracks must belong to assailant."

"Do you think whoever attacked Mr. Blatt was the same person who attacked Mr. Bidwell?" Ellie asked as she carefully stepped around the footprints, letting the deputy guide her. The last thing she wanted to do was mess up evidence.

"Maybe," Liam said. "It's certainly possible. It would be quite a coincidence if the attacks weren't linked, but coincidences do happen so it's never safe to assume something like that."

"If only the first victim's body had been found sooner," Russell said once they were inside the building. "Then we might have been able to get footprints in the snow from that crime scene too."

"Did you ever get in touch with Mr. Blatt?" Ellie asked.

"Yes. He's going to come in tomorrow to give a statement."

"That's good." She sighed. "It looks like the pickup window's going to get put on hold again. At least nobody died this time."

"Considering what happened last time, Mr. Blatt was a very lucky man indeed," Russell said. He glanced around the room. "I'll give you a few minutes to see if anything is missing. Liam, you're sure the building is clear?"

"Positive, Sheriff," the deputy said. "There's nothing in here that will hurt Ms. Pacelli."

The sheriff nodded. "All right, I'll take your word for it. Ellie, while you look around, I'll be outside with Liam going over the scene of the attack. If you need anything, holler and I'll be right in."

Alone in the pizzeria, Ellie began her search. She wasn't sure where to start. What would a burglar want to steal the most?

She made a beeline for the cash register, but it was still intact and the cash inside looked untouched. She would make a point of counting it out tomorrow, but she highly doubted that any thief would have taken only a portion of the money inside.

It didn't take too long to check that all of the small hand appliances were still in their proper spots, and that the refrigerators and pantry were just as she had left them. Nothing seemed to be missing or out of place. Once again, someone had been attacked just outside the pizzeria, but there was no obvious link to the restaurant itself.

Maybe it is *Jeffrey or Xavier or someone else from Cheesaroni*, she thought. *The only link between the attacks is the new pickup window. The only problem is, I just can't see why anyone would think that window is important enough to kill over.*

Still puzzling over the mystery, she went back outside to rejoin Russell and Liam. The two men were gazing at the footprints in the snow, wearing near identical expressions of focus. She watched them silently, not wanting to interrupt them. After another minute, Russell stood up. His expression was grim.

"What is it?" she asked, her heart beginning to beat faster. There seemed to be no end to the bad news tonight.

"I'm going to need shoe sizes from each of your employees," he told her.

"You don't think one of them did this?"

"I don't know." He saw her look, and continued before she could say anything. "Ellie, I'm not trying to say one of them is a murderer. I know you like and care about them all. But there are three sets of footprints here. One belongs to Mr. Blatt. These must be his right here…" he pointed to the tracks coming out from the pizzeria. "I'll get his shoe size and a print of his tread in the morning to confirm.

But look at these here..." he gestured to a tangle of footsteps following along the edge of the pizzeria. "Two different people. Which means that either this attack was coordinated, or two people came up to the pizzeria within minutes of each other just before Mr. Blatt left for the night. One set of tracks is much smaller than the other. My guess is those belong to a woman. Whoever attacked the two contractors would have had to know the times that they were going to be here. My guess is the only people who knew that were—"

"Me and my employees," Ellie said, feeling ill. "I don't understand. Why would my employees want to hurt the people working on the pickup window?"

"Have you had a falling out with any of them recently?" he asked. "Any sort of argument, maybe a disagreement over hours or pay?"

"No, nothing like that at all."

"Were any of them unhappy about the addition of the pickup window?"

"No. It was going to make things easier for all of us," she said. "I really don't think there's a motive for any of them to do something like this. Even if we did have a disagreement, or someone wasn't happy about the construction, it's a big jump from being annoyed to actually killing someone."

"Murder is rarely logical," he said. He blew out a sigh, which steamed in the freezing air. "Now, about the flowers. Do they mean anything to you?"

She crouched down to look at the bouquet laying in the snow. The blossoms were white, and reminded her of the sort of arrangement she might see at a funeral. She didn't see a note, or any indication of where the flowers had come from.

"I think this type of flower is supposed to symbolize mourning or something like that," she said. "But beyond that, no, they don't mean anything to me."

"Whoever brought them placed them in the exact spot where Nathan Bidwell's body was found."

Ellie felt a chill at the words that had nothing to do with the frigid night air. "So, whoever dropped them off must have been at the murder scene?"

Russell nodded, but said nothing more. After a moment, he offered her his hand and pulled her to her feet. "I don't think there's anything else that you need to do here," he said. "If it's all right with you, I'll drive you back to your car and see you off. Then I'll come back here and help Liam finish up."

"Okay," she said, still looking down at the flowers. "Just let me know if there's anything else I can do to help."

Something was bothering her, but she wasn't sure what. With any luck, it would come to her later that night. She knew that the sheriff and his deputy would be able to work better with her out of the way; besides, she was getting cold, so she was happy enough to follow Russell back to his truck. She had a lot to think about tonight.

CHAPTER TWELVE

Ellie opened the over just as the timer went off and pulled out a tasty-looking tray of homemade sugar cookies. She nudged the oven shut with her knee so the adventurous and always hungry Bunny wouldn't burn herself, then slid the tray onto a cooling rack on the counter. The kitchen was pleasantly warm, and the cozy atmosphere was only heightened by the slowly falling snowflakes outside.

"I can't wait to try one of those with icing on it," Shannon said, eyeing the cookie tray. "Homemade cookies with homemade icing… you can't beat that."

"I'm sure by the time Christmas is over, we'll all be sick of these cookies," Ellie said. "We may have made just a tad too many."

The two women turned to look at the three balls of cookie dough remaining on the counter. That was only the sugar cookie dough—they still had peanut butter dough in the fridge for buckeye cookies, as well as dough for gingerbread people. Ellie was planning on donating a good amount of the cookies to the sheriff's department, along with her gift of a new coffee machine, but they would still be left with far more cookies than they could ever eat on their own.

"I think I'll freeze most of mine," her friend said. "Christmas cookies taste just as good when eaten in the summer, after all."

"That's true," Ellie said with a laugh. "Let's get the next batch started, then I'm going to bring some of this eggnog out to Nonna."

It was a few days after the second attack at the pizzeria. She hadn't heard any new from Russell about the case, though she had the feeling that there was something he wasn't telling her. Things had settled back down at the pizzeria, and even though the window still hadn't been installed, no one had complained about the chilly kitchen. No matter what Russell said, she just couldn't see one of her employees attacking someone. The four of them had become almost like family to her. They had all been through the ups and downs of the pizzeria together, and she wouldn't insult their loyalty and hard work by treating them like suspects.

Even though things had been going so well at the pizzeria, this afternoon of cookie making with Shannon and her grandmother was just what she needed. Friends and family had become more important to her than ever since she had moved back to Kittiport, and the recent attacks had reminded her just how quickly her loved ones could be taken away from her.

With the second batch of cookies in the oven, the two women took a short break to visit with Ann Pacelli in the living room. Marlowe, who was perched on the back of an easy chair, gave Shannon a wary look before deciding to ignore her. The bird had never been a fan of strangers, but Ellie had noticed that she seemed to accept women more easily than men. It had taken her weeks to win the macaw's trust, but she was glad that she had put the effort in. The parrot was surprisingly intelligent, and was just as much a part of their family as Bunny was.

"I can smell the cookies from here," Nonna said as they joined her on the couch. "They smell heavenly. You two ladies are such skilled bakers. Do you think there will be any left over? I would love to bring some Christmas cookies to my friends who live at the assisted living home."

"We'll have plenty," Ellie told her. "I'll set some aside for them, and for anyone else you want to give cookies to."

"Thank you so much, dear. I feel bad that I'm not in there helping."

"You're still recovering from a broken arm, I'm just happy to see you holding still for once," the pizzeria owner replied. She realized suddenly that she sounded like Russell had after her concussion, when he was always urging her to be careful and take things slowly.

"Ah, this is the life," Shannon said, leaning back into the plush cushions of the couch. "I can't believe it's almost Christmas already, and the parade is this weekend. Time just flies, doesn't it? It seems like yesterday that we were all out sunning ourselves on a boat."

"Before we know it, winter will be over and it will be hot and humid again," Ellie said. "It's easy to forget to enjoy moments like these while they're happening, and they're over so quickly."

"I wish James would slow down and enjoy the season," Shannon said with a sigh. "He just wants the holidays to be over so work will pick up again. After this big job, he's got nothing."

"Speaking of the holidays," Ellie said, "when is your sister arriving? We should all go out to dinner together when she gets here."

"Oh, I didn't tell you? She cancelled the trip," Shannon said. "So, it will just be the three of us on Christmas. Unless Russell has to work, then it will just be James and I."

Ellie and her grandmother exchanged a look. She thought that they might have both just had the same idea at the exact same time, but she wanted to talk to the older woman before saying anything just to be sure.

"Speaking of Russell and his work," her friend carried on, "has he been talking to you at all about the attacks? He won't say a thing to James and me. In fact, he completely clammed up after the second attack. I mean, I know I work for the paper, but I *am* his sister-in-law. He should know that I mean it when I say I won't write down anything that he doesn't want me to."

"We've only spoken a couple of times since Monday night," Ellie said, "and he hasn't said anything to me about the case, either." She hesitated, then decided that it couldn't hurt to share her fears with the two people closest to her. "I think he suspects that one of my employees might have been involved."

Nonna frowned. "He can't really think that. Your grandfather hired all of those marvelous young people, and he wouldn't hire anyone criminal."

Ellie hesitated, then decided not to remind the older woman about Xavier. "He didn't hire Iris," she said instead. "I did. But she's a wonderful girl, and wouldn't hurt a fly."

"I'm sure the sheriff can't honestly think any of them would do something so horrible," the older woman said. "He knows you're a good judge of character, and he respected Arthur an awful lot."

"I don't know," Shannon said. "I'm sure Russell knows you and your granddad wouldn't hire anyone bad on purpose, but he keeps to the facts when he's working on a case. If the evidence points towards someone, he's going to consider them a suspect. It doesn't matter who they know or how well he knows them."

"I just can't see any of them attacking someone," Ellie said. "If he really thinks that one of them could be the killer then doesn't that mean he's wasting his time while the trail to the real killer grows colder and colder?"

"Ellie… I know you trust your employees, but you trust Russell too, don't you?" her friend asked. "I hate to say it, but he's not wrong too often. If he really thinks that the killer could be someone who works at Papa Pacelli's, then maybe you should consider the possibility too."

The pizzeria owner hesitated, remembering her own suspicion when she saw the white bouquet lying in the exact spot where Nathan's body had been found. She pushed the thoughts away as quickly as they came. No, she wasn't even going to entertain the thought.

"I know you mean well, but I just can't see one of them being the killer," she told the other woman. "You don't know them like I do. I see them almost every day."

"I know," Shannon said. She sounded sad. "It's just something to think about. You know—oh, there's the timer. I'll go get the cookies out and put the next batch in. I'll be right back."

While her friend was in the other room, Ellie turned to her grandmother. The two women had a quick conversation. The pizzeria owner was glad to find that she had been right—they were both on the same page.

"I put the next batch of sugar cookies in, but I couldn't figure out how to set the timer, so we'll just have to… what's going on?" Shannon asked as she came back into the room. She looked between the two Pacelli women.

"Nonna and I would like to invite you, James, and Russell to a Christmas Eve dinner here at the house," Ellie told her. "It'll just be us, otherwise. I think we both would prefer a big, festive dinner, though of course there's nothing wrong with just the two of us celebrating if you can't make it."

"I'll have to speak with James, but I'd love to," the other woman said. "What about your father, Ellie? Didn't you say he might join you?"

Nonna sighed. "He ended up deciding not to visit after all. It will be just us Pacelli girls here."

"I'm sorry," Shannon said. "I'll talk to James when I get home, but I'm sure he'll say yes. Thank you both for the invite—it means a lot to me."

"Of course. Christmas is about coming together and spending time with the people you care about," Ellie said. "I can't think of a better way to spend it than surrounded by good friends."

CHAPTER THIRTEEN

The pizzeria, along with every other shop on Main Street, closed early on parade Friday. Ellie had just enough time to run home, change into something warmer than her work clothes, and pick up her grandmother before heading back into town to meet up with Shannon, James, and Russell. Russell had brought enough camping chairs for the five of them, which they set up along the sidewalk in front of the deli.

It seemed as if the entire town had turned out to watch the parade. Everyone was in a festive mood. Groups of carol singers made their way down the road, and vendors were handing out hot cocoa and cider on the corners.

Ellie had planned to see if she could enter a float for the pizzeria into the parade this year, but with everything that had happened in the past few weeks, she simply hadn't had time. Now that she saw just how many people turned out for this annual Kittiport tradition, she regretted not making more of an effort. It would have been wonderful publicity for Papa Pacelli's, not to mention that it would have been tons of fun.

"Next year," she sighed under her breath. Russell looked over at her and she smiled. It was nice to be out with him, not talking about any cases or any work at all for that matter, and just enjoying a fun event together.

Nonna was on the other side of her, bundled up in a warm blanket in her chair. Ever since the elderly woman had broken her arm, she had seemed so much frailer to her granddaughter. Ellie gazed at her for a long moment, trying to remember back to how her grandmother had looked a few months ago, when Ellie had first moved back to the small Maine town. Either the older woman had aged tremendously in the few months since, or she was making less of an effort to hide the effects of her years now that she didn't have to worry about being carted off to a nursing home.

There was no question of leaving the elderly woman on her own, of course. Somehow, without ever really deciding it or talking with her grandmother about it, what had originally been a temporary arrangement while they both got back on their feet had become permanent. Ellie knew that if she moved away, it would be impossible for Nonna to keep living in the big house that she had spent the last half century in, and there was no possible way she could do that to the woman. No, Ellie was here for good… and she didn't mind it in the slightest.

The sound of clapping from down the road signaled the beginning of the parade. At first, Ellie could only hear the music, but within minutes she saw the first display roll slowly down the road. She settled herself into her chair and relaxed to enjoy the show. She knew that she would remember this wonderful night for many years to come.

By the time the parade ended, Ellie was beginning to feel chilled. It was such a beautiful night, and she didn't want it to end yet, so she invited the rest of their small group into the pizzeria for hot mugs of coffee. The dining area was nice and toasty, and with Christmas music playing over the radio, was the perfect place for the five of them to talk. When Ellie returned to the kitchen to get the freshly made coffee, the resulting cold draft turned the conversation inevitably to the unfinished pickup window project.

"I know, I need to get it fixed," Ellie sighed. "I just… well, I don't know if it's safe to hire anyone else. So far both of the contractors I've hired have been attacked. One was killed, and the other was lucky to get away with his life. How could I ask someone else to put their lives at risk like that?"

"You can't just leave that hole in the wall indefinitely," Shannon said. "What if the killer is never caught? Are you just going to leave that plastic hanging up forever?"

"We're going to catch the person responsible for the attacks," Russell said firmly. "Once he or she is safely behind bars, Ellie will be able to get the project finished without worrying about another casualty."

"What if I tied the rest of the project up for her?" James asked. "No, don't look at me like that Russell, I know what you're going to say. I can take care of myself. I'd be willing to stay on the job site with the men until it's done to make sure no one gets hurt. The window's basically ready to install, isn't it?" Ellie nodded. "I've got a guy who does windows, and it shouldn't take him more than a couple of hours to put it in, assuming everything was measured correctly."

"I don't like it," the sheriff said. "I know you think you can handle whatever comes up, but we don't know what we're dealing with here."

"How about you use me as bait?" James said. Seeing the look on their faces, he explained quickly, "If you really think someone's trying to kill Ellie's contractors for whatever reason, then the best way to catch the killer would be to put another contractor on the job and keep a close eye on him, wouldn't it?"

Russell was looking less and less happy by the minute, but he didn't deny anything that his brother had said.

"So just assign one of your deputies to keep an eye on this place while I work. I'll stay on alert too. Best case scenario, the guy makes a move and you nab him. Worst case scenario, Ellie gets a window installed in the kitchen and doesn't have to freeze her fingers off at work anymore."

"Worst case scenario, and we're going to your funeral instead of Christmas dinner," Russell grumbled. He sighed and ran his hand through his hair. Ellie knew him well enough to know that James had won. "I can't tell you what to do. If Ellie agrees to this, I'll get Bethany to park across the street while you're working on the window. She will be under strict orders to call in anything suspicious or out of the ordinary."

James turned to Ellie, and eager look on his face. *He views this as an adventure*, she thought. *What am I supposed to say? If I let him take the job and something happens, Russell will never forgive me. Worse, I'll never forgive myself. But if I say no, we could be losing our best chance to catch a very dangerous person.*

She bit her lip before answering. "Okay," she said at last. "Just be careful, all right?"

"I've got something for you, Ellie," Russell said, pushing his chair back with a scraping sound as he stood up suddenly. "It's in my truck. I'll help you install it tonight if you want."

Glad for the change in topic, she got up and followed him through the kitchen and out the back door, leaving Shannon in charge of making sure everyone had enough coffee. She was curious—what had Russell gotten her? Would it give her a clue into who he thought the killer might be?

"Here," he said, holding up a box. "Motion detectors for the interior of the pizzeria, and a motion-activated night camera for the back door. Both systems will link to your phone and will alert you if an alarm is set off."

"Wow," she said, eyeing the equipment. "This is a serious upgrade from just turning the deadbolt and hoping for the best the way I do now."

He squinted at her. "You do realize that most people would be able to squeeze through that hole in the wall with no problem? Locking the doors isn't going to do anything other than deter a very lazy criminal." The sheriff shook his head. "This won't stop anyone from trespassing onto the premises, of course, but it will at least give you a warning if they do. With any luck, the camera will manage to catch a picture of whoever's behind all of this."

"It's a wonderful idea," she said. "Thank you. I do worry about people breaking in. It will be such a relief to finally have that window installed at last."

"I would agree with you, if it wasn't my brother doing the installing." He shook his head. "If this keeps up, I'm going to have a full head of grey hair by the new year."

CHAPTER FOURTEEN

Russell installed the motion detectors and the camera the next day. Ellie watched him anxiously, helping when she could and worrying all the while about just how expensive the devices had been.

With one motion sensor in the dining area, one in the kitchen, and the camera just outside the employee entrance, she would know if someone intruded at night. The security system linked directly to her phone, and would send her an alert if any of the sensors picked up movement. It wasn't perfect by any means—Russell warned her that the motion sensitive camera outdoors might pick up wandering wildlife as well as people, and of course there was always the fact that she was bound to forget about the alarms and scare herself half to death at some point.

"You can set them to a timer," he explained, "so they'll turn on and off automatically according to the pizzeria's hours. But if you come in after hours, you'll need to access the app and turn them off yourself. And don't forget that they'll turn on automatically half an hour after closing, so you'll have to remember to shut them off if you stay later than usual."

"This is an amazing gift," she told him. "I really appreciate it. You didn't have to go out of your way and do all of this—not only buying them, but also installing everything for me."

"It wasn't a completely altruistic move," he admitted. "I'm going to feel a lot better now that I won't have to worry about you walking in in the middle of a break-in."

"One person can only have so much terrible luck," she said, laughing. "I think I've had my fair share of unlucky encounters by now." More seriously she added, "But really, I don't know how to thank you… Oh! I was going to wait until Christmas, but it's only a few days away anyway. I got something for the sheriff's department that I think you'll appreciate. It's at Nonna's house. If you want to stop by, I'll give it to you this evening. I'll throw in a pizza too, as thanks for all of this."

After a quick test of the new security system after the pizzeria closed for the evening, Ellie hurried home to pack up her gifts for the sheriff's department. By the time Russell got there, she had containers full of homemade cookies waiting for him as well as the box that contained the new coffee machine. If the coffee *still* had that funny taste the next time she visited, she was just going to chalk it up to some sort of curse and give up on drinking anything while she was there.

"These are some of the cookies that Shannon and I made," she told him. "I thought you and the deputies would enjoy them. We made way too many. I've been handing them out left and right, and still have far too many for us to ever finish before they go stale."

"Thanks," he said. "I'm sure everyone will appreciate them."

She showed him the coffee maker next, and was rewarded when he laughed out loud.

"Bethany's going to love you," he said. "Really, we all will. We drink way too much of the stuff whenever we need to stay awake late at night while we're working on a case."

"I figured you'd like having a machine that produces palatable coffee," she said. "I don't know how you've managed to go years drinking that other stuff. You guys do so much for this town, I thought you should at least have some good coffee."

Marlowe, who until then had been watching the two of them silently from inside her cage by the stairway, interrupted them. The macaw's voice was crystal clear when she spoke. "Hi!"

Russell jumped. He looked around the room until his gaze finally settled on the parrot.

"Was that the bird?" he asked.

Ellie nodded. "She doesn't usually talk around strangers. She must like you."

Marlowe repeated herself, then ran her beak across the cage bars.

"That's amazing," the sheriff said, clearly impressed. "She sounds just like a woman."

"You should hear her when she laughs," Ellie said. "It's a bit eerie. She cracks up whenever someone swears, and her laugh sounds just like a person's. Oh, and she's recently begun telling Bunny that she's a 'bad dog!' whenever she sees her."

"You're kidding," he said. "What does Bunny do?"

"Oh, at first, she slunk away whenever she heard Marlowe, but now she just ignores it," she told him. "I'm really amazing that she said anything in front of you. Normally she completely ignores visitors, or if she really doesn't like them, she screams at them. And that is not a pretty sound."

"I'm glad I got to hear her talk. I always hear about talking parrots, but it's even more impressive in person. I never guessed she would sound so human."

Marlowe's interruption had gotten their conversation was off track. Ellie was trying to remember what they had been talking about when her phone let out a loud series of beeps. She didn't recognize the unfamiliar noise at first.

"It's the pizzeria," she exclaimed when she finally made the connection. "One of the alarms is going off."

Russell looked over her shoulder as she pulled up the app and swiped through it to figure out which device had been triggered. It was the outdoor camera. It had snapped a few pictures of a hooded form depositing something unidentifiable in the snow on the ground next to the employee entrance. Ellie felt goosebumps at the sight. What was going on?

"I'm going to go see what's up," the sheriff said. "Thanks for the gifts for the department. I'll give you a call if I find out who that is."

"What are you talking about?" Ellie asked. "I'm going with you, of course."

Russell's heavy truck handled the snowy roads effortlessly, and the two of them made good time to town. Even though he had pushed the speed limit, they were too late to catch whoever the mysterious figure had been. However, the mysterious object in the snow was still there—it was another bunch of flowers.

The sheriff crouched in front of them and frowned. Ellie, whose curiosity had been sated once she saw that once again there was no note, watched him from the warmth of the truck. Was the person bringing the flowers connected to the killer somehow? *Maybe they're the same person*, she thought. *Maybe whoever attacked Nathan hadn't meant to kill him, and feels bad about it now.* She dismissed the theory almost immediately; Russell had said there had been multiple sets of footprints in the snow the night that Mr. Blatt had been attacked. That probably meant that the killer and the flower person were different people.

This just keeps going around in circles, she thought. *We're never going to catch anyone at this rate. James can't begin installing the window until after Christmas, so there's no chance this thing will be solved before the holiday.*

Russell came back to the car and held his hands in front of the heat vent. "I don't know what's going on, Ellie, but I don't like it," he said. "Something's off with this case. I feel like I'm missing something important."

"You've gone over everything," she said. "Multiple times. I don't think you're missing anything."

"I just wish I knew what was going on," he said, grinding his teeth.

"Me too," she said. "I don't like this anymore that you do. Whoever is behind all of this seems to be at least one step ahead."

"That, or they're just darned lucky," he said. "Either way, it's making them extremely difficult to catch."

CHAPTER FIFTEEN

"They're going to be here in three hours," Ellie moaned to her grandmother, an edge of panic in her voice. "We have so much left to do."

"We are perfectly on schedule," Nonna said. "Besides, it's Christmas Eve. Why not relax a bit? No one is going to be upset if dinner is a few minutes late."

She knew the older woman was right. It was a dinner with family and friends. There was no reason to stress herself over it, but she couldn't help the feeling that everything had to be perfect. Perhaps the recent sleepless nights had caught up with her at last. The alarm on her phone had gone off at least twice since Russell had installed the security system. Someone had obviously taken to visiting the pizzeria at night, but they still didn't know who or why.

"I need to get the ham in, at least," she said, trying to focus on the present moment. "I need it to be out in time to put the cheesy potatoes and green bean casserole in the oven before dinner. I don't think all three will fit at once."

The ham was huge, and a bit intimidating. She had improved her cooking skills immeasurably since working at the pizzeria, but was by no means as experienced as Nonna or even Shannon. If they were having pizza for dinner, she would be confident, but a ham was a whole different story.

She had wrestled the thing into the oven and begun peeling the potatoes when the now-familiar sound of the alarm sounded from her phone. "Not again," she said. She set down the peeler and picked up the phone. The image that the camera had snapped was too snowy to give her any answers. She was tempted to ignore it; it was Christmas Eve, after all, and the mysterious person hadn't done any harm any of the other times he or she had appeared. For all she knew, there might not be anyone there. She wondered if it was possible for snow to set off the sensitive motion sensor. The wind was really gusting out there, blowing the large flakes into every crevice it could reach.

The temptation to ignore the alarm wasn't stronger than her urge to catch the killer, so she made the tough decision to give Russell a call. She knew it would be what he wanted. She just hoped that it really was just the snow, and that he'd still be there in time for dinner.

After getting off the phone with the sheriff, she returned to the potatoes. She managed to get through the entire pile before being interrupted by her phone again. When she saw Russell's number, she fully expected him to be calling to give her the all clear. She was shocked when he answered her cheerful greeting with a grim pronouncement.

"Ellie, you better get down here. I've got to warn you: you're not going to like it."

The drive to town through the snow and wind was painfully slow. All the Christmas cheer—along with the pressure she had felt to create a flawless meal—was gone, replaced by a cold sense of dread. Russell hadn't told her much, though he had assured her that no one was hurt. She was grateful for that, but wished he had told her more. Was the pizzeria okay? Had it been broken into? She had so many questions, but there was no question of her risking a phone call while trying to navigate the snowy roads.

After what seemed like an eternity, she pulled into a parking space next to Russell's truck behind Papa Pacelli's. The kitchen door was propped open, and light was streaming out. *That's odd*, she thought. *Why is he in there?*

She pushed her way into the kitchen and froze mid-step. Iris, her expression subdued, was seated at the table across from Russell. She had her arms crossed, and was gazing at the floor.

"What's going on?" Ellie asked.

Russell met her gaze. He looked sad, not at all triumphant to have been right.

"I found Iris here," he said simply.

"Outside?" she asked.

He nodded. "Her footprints match the ones in the snow from the evening that Mr. Blatt was attacked," he said. "I'm sorry, Ellie, but I need to take her in. I thought you should be the first to know."

"I don't understand," Iris said. "What's going on?"

Ellie couldn't even look at her employee. She felt betrayed, and sick to her stomach at the thought of how many times she had defended the young woman sitting in front of her. It all fit; Iris had known the contractor's schedule, the same as all of her other employees. She had been the one to find both the murder weapon and the body at the first crime scene, and had acted weird ever since. She must have been the one to leave the flowers too, in the exact spot where Nathan had died. The only unsolved piece of the puzzle that remained was motive. Why had Iris killed Nathan Bidwell in the first place?

"I didn't do anything," the young woman said, beginning to sound panicked. "Whatever it is, I didn't do it."

"What were you doing here tonight?" Russell asked her.

Her face grew red.

"If you have a good reason for sneaking around the scene of a murder in the middle of the night, I encourage you to share it sooner, rather than later," the sheriff said. "We just want the truth, that's all."

Iris took a deep breath. "I was giving him flowers, all right?"

"Why?" Ellie was unable to help herself. Her employee hadn't seemed too upset about the murder after it happened. What had happened to make her care so much that she would leave flowers for him at the scene of his death multiple times in one week?

"I met his family," the young woman admitted. "I went to the vigil for him. I don't know why, I guess I felt connected somehow because I'm the one that found his body."

"So, you felt bad for his family and decided to bring flowers for him?" Ellie asked. "Why not give the flowers to his family instead of leaving them in the snow?"

"I didn't feel bad for his family," Iris said. The pizzeria owner and the sheriff traded a surprised look. "They were horrible," she continued. "I talked to one of his relatives. Apparently he and his wife were separated and she was living with her boyfriend, and the kids were all on their cellphones, and… I don't know, I just felt so *bad* for him. He *died* and no one seemed to care. So, I decided to bring him flowers for each person in his family who should have, but wasn't going to."

She fell silent, and neither Ellie nor Russell spoke right away. The only sound was the rustling of the plastic over the place where the window should go as the wind tugged at it.

Something about her story rings true, she thought. *But can I really believe it?* She just didn't know. Iris was the newest of her employees, and she knew the least about her. She glanced at Russell, who appeared to be deep in thought.

"Please, Ms. P., you've gotta believe me. I know I probably should have told you about the flowers, but I was embarrassed, and you never said anything about them, so I thought maybe you knew somehow."

It was true that she hadn't mentioned the flowers to any of her employees. She hadn't wanted to concern them unnecessarily. In retrospect, maybe she should have said something. If what Iris was saying was the truth, then it could have saved them a lot of time and effort.

"Do you have anyone who can corroborate your story?" Russell asked.

"My sister," Iris said immediately. "I told her all about the dead man and the flowers—everything."

"Would you be willing to come down to the station and answer a few more questions while we see if we can get in touch with her?"

She nodded. "Definitely. I didn't mean to cause all this trouble. I'm sorry."

"If your story holds up, then I'll be the one apologizing," he told her. "I must have given you quite the scare."

"When I saw you coming towards me through the snow, I thought you might have been the killer at first," she admitted with a nervous laugh. "I thought I was going to be murdered, on Christmas Eve and everything."

"Right, shoot, it's Christmas Eve," Russell said. He gave Ellie an apologetic look. "I don't know if I'll be able to make it to dinner on time."

"I know, it's fine," she told him.

"Am I in trouble, Ms. Pacelli?" Iris asked.

"No," Ellie told her, trying to sound reassuring. "If all you were doing was leaving flowers for a dead man, I think that's sweet. You won't be in any trouble for an act of kindness. Just come in the day after tomorrow like normal, once Russ—the sheriff releases you."

Russell stood up. “Well, the sooner we go, the sooner we’ll be done,” he said. “I don’t know about you, but I’m eager to finish up with all of this and enjoy the rest of my Christmas Eve.”

CHAPTER SIXTEEN

Ellie shut her car door and sat in the dark, thinking about everything that had just happened. She was relieved, of course—Iris wasn't the killer, that much was clear. She didn't think she was lying, but perhaps most importantly, Russell seemed to think she was telling the truth, too. She trusted his judgment when it came to this sort of thing.

Ellie was also embarrassed. She had been so quick to assume the worst of the young woman. All her big talk about trusting her employees had gone right out the window. She could only hope that Iris would forgive her.

As she thought of ways to cheer the young woman up, she remembered the small pile of gifts that she had in the trunk of her car. She had finally managed to complete all her holiday shopping, including getting something for each of her employees. She might as well bring the gifts inside now, while she was here. It would be a nice surprise for them to find their gifts waiting for them when they came into work the morning after Christmas.

Bracing herself against the cold, Ellie popped the trunk and hurried around to the back of the vehicle to take the small pile of presents out. For a precarious moment, she fumbled with her keys, almost dropping them twice as she struggled to find the right one to unlock the employee entrance door.

Inside, she carried the gifts to the counter and set them down carefully. She hadn't gotten anything too expensive for them, but had tried to match each gift to something unique about her employees.

Jacob and Clara, who did most of the delivery driving, each got unique hats with a headlamp and their name on them. Rose, who seemed to enjoy working at the cash register the most, got an apron with special pockets for her phone and an order pad. Iris had been the hardest to shop for, since she was the newest employee, but Ellie had eventually settled on a personalized apron for her as well.

Ellie set the boxes and bags up on the small round table in the kitchen, then took a step back and smiled. There! Now they would have a pleasant surprise when they came in the day after tomorrow. And the day after that, James would be installing the window. Things were beginning to look up for all of them. There was still plenty of time for her, Russell, and Iris all to get home and enjoy the rest of the evening.

A slow, creaking sound made the pizzeria owner jump. She glanced towards the door, and realized it was just the wind pushing it open. It must not have latched properly behind her when she came in with all of the gifts.

Deciding it was time to go, anyway, she took one last look at the row of gifts on the table, then grabbed her keys off the counter and pulled the door open the rest of the way. What she saw made her yelp in fear and leap backwards.

A man was standing in the doorway, perfectly silhouetted against the snow and dark outside. He was tall and thin, with a worn-out coat. She knew she had seen him before, but couldn't figure out where. There were more pressing questions—like what he was doing in her doorway.

"Sorry," the man said, a note of surprise in his own voice. He had a large bag in one hand, and was wearing thin leather gloves. "I didn't mean to startle you, Ms. Pacelli."

"That's okay," she said automatically. "Do I know you?"

"George Walsh," he said, his brows drawing together. "We met a few weeks ago…"

"I remember," she said, her meeting with him coming back to her in a rush. He had been the last contractor she had met with before making her decision. "I'm sorry, but what are you doing here?"

"I've come to see if you've reconsidered," he said. Something about the way he tightened his grip on the black bag at his side sent a warning rushing through her body. Every muscle was on high alert.

"Reconsidered what?" she asked, trying to figure out which way was up on the pepper spray without looking down at her keys.

"Hiring me," he said. "I heard you were in the market for another contractor. This window isn't going to install itself, after all."

"If you want to talk about that, we can set up a time later this week," she said, keeping her voice as bright and cheery as possible. "It's Christmas Eve, and I have to get home to my family."

"Well, since we're both here now, it seems like we might as well take advantage of the situation and have a chat."

The conversation was becoming absurd. Ellie's heart was pounding in her chest, yet she had a smile plastered on her face and was chatting with this man as if they had run into each other at a coffee shop.

"Really, I would prefer to reschedule," she said. "I have a ham in the oven at home, and I'll need to take it out soon."

"I insist," George said. His tone left no room for debate.

Tightening her grip on the pepper spray, Ellie took a slow step backwards. She didn't have a choice, but every cell in her body was screaming at her not to let him in. She wasn't sure how or why he was connected to the attacks, but she was certain that he was.

George followed her into the kitchen and shut the door firmly behind him. Something sloshed in his bag.

"Take a seat," he suggested. She did so, trying to do what she could to keep him happy until she came up with a better idea.

"Well," she said, still striving to sound normal. "What was it you wanted to discuss?"

He blinked and looked from her to his bag. "You see," he began, licking his lips nervously. "You see, I'm in a tough spot. I really needed the money from this job. I thought you were gonna hire me. You seemed nice, ya know?"

"Well, I could still hire you," Ellie said. "Do you want the job?"

"It's gone too far for that," George said. He sounded sad, which surprised her.

"What do you mean?" she asked.

He gazed at her for a long moment, as if weighing his options. At last, he sighed and shook his head. "I really didn't want to hurt anyone else. I was sure that this place would be empty. That's why I chose Christmas Eve to do it. Everyone's home with their families, no one's eating out at a pizza place. You definitely weren't supposed to be here."

"What were you going to do, George?" she asked, trying to remember how Karen said she talked to her more difficult patients. She kept them engaged, and tried to find a way to reason with them.

"Listen, I'm not a bad person," he said. "You've got to understand that. I really need the money. And I didn't mean to hurt you."

"You haven't hurt me," she said. "Not yet." Her eyes flicked towards the door. She doubted she could reach it and get it open in time.

"I'm sorry, Ms. Pacelli. You seem like a nice woman. I'm going to have to ask you to stand up and walk over to that pantry now."

"I'm not doing that." She tightened her grip on the pepper spray, mentally preparing herself to blast him in the face and then take off.

"I'm asking you nicely. Don't make me ask you again."

He shifted and she tensed, ready to make her move the second he came closer. Instead of approaching her, however, he reached into the interior of his jacket and withdrew a small black gun. Ellie felt a rush of fear. There was no way her pepper spray could help her stand up to someone with a firearm.

"Into the pantry," he said. "Now."

She had no choice. Terrified, and still having no idea what was going to happen, she did as she was told. George shut the pantry door behind her. There was the sound of something sliding across the floor, and then the handle jiggled. She realized he must have just improvised some sort of doorstop; the pantry didn't have a lock.

Ellie tried to slow her breathing and think. Was there anything in the pantry that she could use to save herself? No, definitely not. A room full of food was completely useless to her now. She still had her pepper spray and keys, at least, but neither of those things would do her any good either.

"George?" she called. "Mr. Walsh?"

No answer. She pressed her ear to the door to try and hear what he was doing. At first, she couldn't hear anything, but after a moment she picked up a soft sloshing sound. *What could he possibly be—oh my goodness, he's going to burn the place down.* Along with the realization came a rush of terror stronger than she had ever felt before. She did not want to be burned alive.

"Help!" she screamed. "Let me out!"

She pounded on the door, but George ignored her. Realizing that her efforts were futile, she stopped and tried to calm herself down. She was on the verge of hyperventilating, and tears stung her eyes.

"My phone," she said aloud, struck by a bolt of hope. Frantically, she patted her pockets, but to no avail. She had probably left the cellphone on the passenger seat of her car where it would do her absolutely no good.

Ellie pressed her ear to the door again, trying to listen. She heard nothing for a couple of minutes until her ears caught a slight crackling sound. A moment later, she smelled smoke.

"Please," she called. "Let me out."

There was no answer. She didn't know if George had left, or if he was standing out there listening to her beg. She knew by now that he must be the killer. Somewhere in his twisted mind, he must have decided that if he killed the competition, then she would have to hire him. But why the fire? *He said he needed money*, she thought. *Maybe he hoped that I would hire him to repair the fire damage. He did say he didn't plan on my being here.*

Even if he hadn't originally planned to burn her alive, it didn't really matter right now. She was locked in a pantry, and her kitchen was on fire. She could only hope that George wasn't experienced with arson. If he knew what he was doing, she would be burnt to a crisp long before the firetrucks got there.

The smoke began to make her cough. It was seeping into the pantry at an alarming rate. She remembered learning about fire safety years ago, but somehow, she didn't think putting a wet towel under the door would help in this situation, even if she had one.

Ellie retreated to the back corner of the room and crouched down on the floor, trying to inhale as little smoke as possible. Nothing seemed to work. The burning in her lungs only increased, no matter how shallow she kept her breaths.

She realized that if she just sat there and waited for help, she would die. She climbed to her feet and felt her way to the door. The doorknob was warm, but not hot. The fire must not have caught too well, and was producing mostly smoke. That was good; at least if she could get the door open, she wouldn't be stumbling into a raging inferno.

Ellie turned the knob and pushed. The door moved a fraction of an inch, but then got caught up on whatever George had used to block it. She took a deep breath, gagged, and tried taking several shallow breaths inside as she prepared herself. Then she slammed against the door with all her might, not caring if she went flying on the other side as long as the door opened.

The door scraped open a few inches further; a disappointing amount, but better than nothing. She body-slammed it again and again until at last it gave way. She stumbled out into the kitchen, coughing and choking on the smoke. She could barely see, but she knew the place well enough by now that she could have navigated it blind.

She had no words for the relief she felt when she finally opened the door to the parking lot. Breathing in the cold fresh air was the most wonderful sensation that she had ever experienced. She fell to her knees in the snow and just breathed until she began to feel lightheaded.

Don't hyperventilate just yet, she told herself. *George is getting away.* Somehow, she was still holding onto her keys. She hit the button to unlock the car, and staggered towards the resulting beep. If her phone wasn't on the front seat, she didn't know what she would do. She'd just have to cross that bridge when she came to it.

Just as her fingers hooked under the door latch, she felt a warm hand come down on her shoulder. She spun around, almost falling, to see George's tall figure through her tearing eyes. His face was ruddy, as if he had stood too close to the fire when he lit it.

"How'd you get out?" he growled. Ellie saw his hand move out of the corner of her eye and remembered the gun. Acting on instinct, she brought her keychain up and depressed the trigger on her bottle of pepper spray.

George gave an agonized howl and fell back, clawing at his eyes. His cries of pain quickly turned into a rasping, hacking cough as he inhaled the chemicals that she had just sprayed at him. He dropped the gun somewhere in the snow, and Ellie took her chance. She yanked the car door open and groped madly across the seat for her phone. She nearly cried with relief when she felt it. Her hands were shaking so much that it took her two tries to pull up her recent calls list, but at long last she got through to Russell.

"There's a fire at the pizzeria," she said, her voice hoarse. "And I caught the killer."

EPILOGUE

Ellie still smelled slightly of smoke when she sat down for Christmas dinner the next day, even though she had washed her hair more times than she could count. Her throat hurt and she had a cough, but none of that spoiled her good mood. It felt marvelous just to be alive.

The dinner the evening before had been cancelled, of course; between the chaos at the pizzeria and Ellie's trip to the hospital for smoke inhalation, they wouldn't have been able to begin eating until well past midnight. She was glad that they were still having a Christmas get together, even though the ham was reheated and the salad was slightly soggy. As far as she was concerned, it was the perfect end to a grueling month.

George Walsh was currently sitting in a holding cell in the Kittiport sheriff's department. He was set to be transferred the next day, and would be awaiting his court date in a jail cell far away from her.

With one charge of murder, two of attempted murder, and one for arson, he was sure to be put away for a long time.

Ellie had come through the fire not too much worse for the wear; sadly, the same couldn't be said about the pizzeria. The smoke damage in the kitchen was extensive, and repairing it would be a long process. She felt a surge of sadness whenever she thought of the kitchen, but it was hard to stay down for too long when she knew that she was lucky just to have escaped with her life.

Russell was staring at her from across the table, worry etched into his expression. She smiled at him, trying to reassure him that she was all right. He had been beside himself the night before when he arrived in the pizzeria parking lot to find her half-unconscious in her car, just feet from a killer and a burning building. She thought he still looked a bit pale.

Shannon and James were at the other end of the table, talking animatedly to each other; every bit the happy couple. James had already offered to have his company do the repair work, for which she was grateful. If she had only gone with his company in the first place, none of this mess would have happened at all.

Ann was seated at the head of the table, carefully cutting her ham. Around her neck she wore Ellie's gift to her: a white gold locket, inside of which was an old photo of her husband along with a photo of her two children. She had teared up when she'd opened the box, and had given Ellie a wordless hug that said more than any thanks ever could.

All in all, Ellie decided, it wasn't a bad Christmas. She was able to spend it with all of the people she had come to care deeply about over the past few months, as well as the animals that brightened her life every day. Bunny was roaming under the table, looking for scraps, and Marlowe was in the other room eating a modified version of Christmas dinner out of her bowl. Both of them had gotten Christmas gifts of their favorite treats, and would probably have gained ten pounds each by tomorrow.

"Merry Christmas," she said, raising her champagne glass. "I know I already said it to everyone, but I just wanted to say it again. This has always been one of my favorite holidays, and the chance to spend it with all of you has only made it better."

"Merry Christmas," the others rang out. There was a clink as they touched their glasses together in a toast. Ellie knew that her life wasn't perfect—far from it, in fact—and there would be a lot of challenges in her way this coming year, but one thing she was certain of; throughout all of it, these people seated at the table with her today would be by her side no matter what.

Made in the USA
Lexington, KY
10 September 2018